LAAL HOLI MEIN UNHOLY - VARDAAN

RAKTIM MUKHERJEE

Made with ♥ on the Notion Press Platform
www.notionpress.com

Om Namah Shivaya, Jay Mahakal, Har Har Mahadev.

To God,

For every blessing I did not deserve, every lesson I did not understand when it arrived, and every path You illuminated when darkness seemed endless.

To my parents,

For giving me life, values, courage, and the freedom to dream beyond my circumstances. Whatever I have achieved, and whatever I may achieve, has its roots in your sacrifices, love, and unwavering faith in me.

To my English teacher, Mr. Subir Lahiri, for teaching me that words can transform imagination into reality.

To my friends, for their patience, encouragement, and unwavering companionship through the years.

And to those who doubted me, who believed I could never succeed—thank you.

This book stands as a testament to the power of perseverance, proving that determination can outlast doubt and turn the impossible into reality.

This book is dedicated to all of you.

— Raktim Mukherjee

Contents

Contents

Foreword

Every story begins with a question.

For me, that question was simple: What survives when everything else is taken away?

Over the years, I have been fascinated by the lives of people who carry the weight of legacy—individuals born into histories they never chose, yet are forced to live, fight, and sometimes die for. From that curiosity emerged Laal Holi Mein Unholy.

This is not merely a story about crime, power, or revenge. At its heart, it is a story about family, loyalty, ambition, sacrifice, and the scars left behind by choices made across generations. It is a tale of kings without crowns, brothers divided by fate, and an empire built on blood and buried beneath betrayal.

As you turn these pages, I invite you to step into a world where every victory has a cost, every loyalty is tested, and every legacy demands a price.

Welcome to the Singh Empire.

Preface

Stories often begin with a character. Sometimes they begin with an event. Laal Holi Mein Unholy began with a question that stayed with me for years:

> "*Can a man outrun the legacy he was born into?*"

The idea of Vardaan emerged from that question. I was fascinated by the contrast between two worlds—a man who looks toward the stars and dreams of exploration, yet belongs to a family rooted in power, violence, and history. The more I explored that conflict, the larger the story became. What started as a tale of revenge gradually transformed into a multi-generational saga about family, loyalty, ambition, love, betrayal, and the burdens we inherit.

Part I, Vardaan, is the beginning of that journey. It follows a man who leaves home to escape a curse, only to discover that some destinies wait patiently for our return. While the world of this novel is fictional, its emotions are not. The characters are driven by fears, hopes, loyalties, and flaws that are deeply human.

As you enter the world of the Singh Empire, I invite you to look beyond the violence and power struggles and discover the people trapped within them.

This is where the story begins.

— Raktim Mukherjee

Prologue

The Curse of Red Earth

There are places where history is written in books. And then there are places where history is written in blood. The Singh Belt belonged to the latter.

Stretching across the coal-dark districts of Jharkhand, through the transport arteries of Bihar, touching the political battlegrounds of eastern Uttar Pradesh and the desert highways of Rajasthan, there existed an invisible kingdom.

No map acknowledged it. No constitution recognized it. Yet everyone knew it existed. Ministers knew. Police officers knew. Contractors knew. Businessmen knew. Even criminals knew. People simply called it—The Empire.

An empire built on coal. On land. On Bricks. On loyalty. On fear. And above all, on legacy.

The story began more than forty years earlier when two friends, more than brothers, arrived in the region with nothing except courage and hunger. Vairav Singh. Jay Singh Bajwa. Together they fought bandits. Together they protected villages. Together they built businesses where others saw wastelands. Their names spread from district to district like folklore. The poor worshipped them. The powerful respected them. The dangerous feared them. But every empire carries within itself the seed of its destruction.

Sometimes that seed is greed. Sometimes power. Sometimes love. And sometimes, it is the quiet jealousy growing inside the heart of a brother. Nobody remembered the exact day the curse began. Some believed it started when Jay Singh Bajwa fell in love with a woman he could never have. Others believed it started when Vairav became larger than the empire itself. The truth had long been buried beneath decades of violence. What remained were consequences. Fathers burying sons. Brothers betraying brothers.

Friends becoming executioners. And every year, when Holi arrived and clouds of red color filled the air, the people of the Singh Belt remembered one thing: The color of celebration and the color of blood looked exactly the same.

CHAPTER ONE

THE MAN AMONG STARS

Pasadena, California, February, 2019.

The stars looked different in America. Vardaan Singh had spent almost eighteen years convincing himself of that. The sky above Pasadena was cleaner. Quieter. Detached from memory. When he looked upward here, he saw possibilities. When he looked upward back home, he remembered ghosts. The observation deck stood nearly empty at this hour.

Beyond the glass walls, the city shimmered beneath a blanket of lights. Highways glowed like rivers of gold. The distant mountains rested beneath a pale silver moon. Above everything stretched the infinite darkness of space. Vardaan preferred that darkness. Space never lied. Numbers never betrayed. Physics never changed because of greed, politics, or family. People did. Always.

At thirty-five, Dr. Vardaan Singh had become one of the most respected aerospace systems specialists in the United States. His research papers were cited internationally. Government agencies sought his expertise. Universities invited him to speak. Several of his projects had already become critical components of future deep-space exploration programs.

The boy who once stared at the night sky from a small village rooftop in India had traveled farther than anyone around him had ever imagined. He had won. At least that was what he kept telling himself. He had escaped. Escaped the empire. Escaped the violence. Escaped the expectations. Escaped the Singh name. Most importantly, he had escaped the destiny that had consumed every man in his family. Or so he believed.

A soft electronic chime interrupted his thoughts. The simulation console behind him flashed green. Results completed. Vardaan walked back toward the workstation. Lines of data filled the screen. Complex calculations. Propulsion models. Trajectory forecasts. Beautiful. Orderly. Predictable. The universe is reduced to mathematics. He smiled. The kind of smile that appeared only when he was working. Only when he forgot who he was.

—Doctor Singh?

He turned. A young researcher stood in the doorway holding a tablet. Emily Parker. One of the brightest engineers on the team. She looked exhausted. Which meant she had probably been working all night.

— Please tell me that's good news,

Vardaan said. Emily grinned.

—We solved the instability issue.

For a moment Vardaan simply stared. Then he laughed. A genuine laugh. Rare, and unexpected. Months of work, hundreds of failed simulations, countless sleepless nights. Finally solved. Emily placed the tablet on the desk.

—We should celebrate.

—We should verify first.

—You sound exactly like a scientist.

—I am a scientist.

—Exactly my point.

Both of them laughed. The room felt lighter. For a brief moment, everything felt exactly as it should. Then his phone vibrated. The sound was small, insignificant. Yet something inside him immediately tightened. Unknown international number. India. His smile disappeared. Emily noticed.

—You okay?

—Yeah.

He wasn't. The phone continued vibrating. He rejected the call. A few seconds later it rang again. Unknown number. Same country code. India. The knot in his stomach grew. Emily quietly picked up her tablet.

—I'll leave you to it.

Vardaan nodded absentmindedly. The room fell silent again. The phone stopped ringing. Then started once more. And once more. And once more. Nobody called like this unless something was wrong. Very wrong. Slowly, he picked up the device. For several seconds he simply stared at the screen. Then he answered.

—Hello?

Nothing. Only breathing. Heavy breathing. An old man's breathing. The sound instantly transported him across continents and decades. Back to dusty courtyards. Back to monsoon evenings. Back to childhood. Back home. His chest tightened.

—Hello?

The breathing continued. Then finally a voice emerged. Broken. Trembling. Barely recognizable.

—Chhote Malik...

Vardaan froze. Ramdeen. The family's oldest caretaker. A man who had worked for the Singhs longer than Vardaan had been alive. A man who practically raised him. A man who never cried. Never.

—Ramdeen?

No response. Only sobbing. The old man was trying to speak. Failing. Trying again. Failing again. Fear began spreading through Vardaan's body. Cold, relentless, primitive.

—Ramdeen, he said quietly.

—What happened?

The answer did not come immediately. Only silence. And somehow that silence felt worse than any words. Outside the glass walls, the California skyline remained unchanged. Cars moved, lights flickered. People lived their lives. Entirely unaware that a universe was collapsing. Finally, Ramdeen managed to speak.

—Chhote Malik...

His voice cracked.

—Vikram Baba...

The name alone was enough. Vardaan stopped breathing. Something was wrong. Terribly wrong.

—...maar diye gaye.

Killed. The words echoed through his mind. But they made no sense. Not at first. Killed? Who? Vikram? No. Impossible. Vikram Singh did not die. Vikram Singh survived. That was what he had always done. Survived riots. Survived attacks. Survived ambushes. Survived politics. Survived betrayal. Vikram survived everything.

That was who he was. A mountain. A fortress. A man who seemed too large to be defeated by ordinary mortality. Killed? No. The words refused to fit reality.

—Ramdeen...

His voice sounded distant. Unfamiliar.

—Tum yeh kya anab shanaab bol rahe ho?

The old man began crying openly now, on the other side of the world, thousands of miles away. Inside a house that suddenly felt haunted.

—Woh log Goli mar di unko, Malik...

Silence.

The room spun. Not physically. Emotionally. Like gravity itself had shifted. Vardaan lowered himself into the nearest chair. His hands were trembling. He hadn't noticed until now. Across the desk stood a framed photograph. A rare personal item. The only one he kept in his office. Two brothers. One older, one younger. A photograph taken years ago.

Vikram had his arm around Vardaan's shoulder. Both smiling. Neither aware of the future waiting for them. Vardaan stared at the image. Unable to look away. Unable to process what he had heard. Memories began surfacing. Uninvited. Relentless. *"Vikram teaching him how to ride a bicycle". "Vikram helping him study". "Vikram shielding him during fights". "Vikram standing between him and their father's expectations"*. "Vikram secretly encouraging his dreams of becoming a scientist". Most people thought the brothers were different. They weren't. Vikram simply carried the burdens so

Vardaan wouldn't have to. The empire. The enemies. The violence. The responsibilities. Everything. Including the future. Especially the future.

Years ago, when Vardaan received admission offers from American universities, their father opposed the decision. The empire needed heirs. The family needed successors. The Singh legacy needed continuation. Only Vikram supported him. Only Vikram fought for him. Only Vikram understood.

—You belong up there, Vikram had said one night while pointing toward the stars.

—And you? Vardaan had asked.

Vikram smiled.

—I belong down here.

The memory shattered him. Because now Vikram is gone. And suddenly there was nobody standing between Vardaan and the world he had spent eighteen years escaping. The empire. The family. The curse. Ramdeen's voice returned through the phone.

—Aap ghar wapis kab aa rahe ho, Chhote Malik?

"Ghar". The word felt like a knife. He looked through the glass wall again. Above California, countless stars burned silently. The same stars he had dedicated his life to studying. The same stars that once represented freedom. Now they felt impossibly distant. Because somewhere beyond oceans and continents, beyond coal mines and highways and forgotten villages, an empire was mourning its king. And the kingdom was waiting for its lost prince to return. Vardaan closed his eyes. For the first time in eighteen years, he already knew the answer. The past had finally found him. And this time, it wasn't asking. It was calling him home.

CHAPTER TWO

THE LONG FLIGHT HOME

Pasadena – Dubai – India, February, 2019.

The airport looked exactly the same as it always had. Crowded. Bright. Indifferent. Hundreds of people moved through the terminal carrying luggage, coffee cups, laptops, children, dreams, disappointments, and destinations. Nobody knew who Vardaan Singh was. Nobody knew his brother had been murdered twelve hours ago. Nobody knew that an empire was waiting for him. And nobody knew that with every passing mile, a man who had spent eighteen years building a new identity was slowly being dragged back into an older one. A far more dangerous one. Vardaan sat beside the departure gate staring through the massive glass windows. Outside, aircraft taxied beneath the evening sky.

The world continued moving. As it always did. Death never stopped the world. Only the people left behind. His phone remained silent now. Ramdeen had called several more times. Each conversation was shorter than the previous one. The old caretaker sounded exhausted. Broken. As if he had aged ten years overnight. The final conversation lasted less than a minute.

—Sab intezaar karat baa, Chhote Malik.

Everyone is waiting.

—Kaun?

A pause. Then the old man answered.

—Ghar...

Home.

—Log...

The people.

—Aur Vikram Baba...

And Vikram.

The line disconnected shortly afterward. Since then, Vardaan had spoken to nobody. Not colleagues. Not friends. Not even himself. Because the moment he allowed himself to think about Vikram, the reality became unbearable. Boarding was announced. Passengers began moving toward the gate. Vardaan stood. Picked up his bag. And walked toward the aircraft. Toward India. Toward the past. Toward the curse.

Several hours later, the lights inside the aircraft dimmed. Most passengers slept. Some watched movies. Others stared blankly into the darkness beyond the windows. Vardaan did neither. He sat awake. Motionless. A half-finished glass of water rested beside him. His eyes remained fixed on the darkness outside. Thirty-seven thousand feet above the earth. Closer to the stars than he had ever been. Yet feeling farther from himself than ever before. The engines hummed softly. A constant mechanical heartbeat. Steady. Predictable. Unlike memory. Memory arrived without warning. And once it arrived, it never asked permission.

The first thing Vardaan remembered was rain. Monsoon rain. Heavy. Relentless. Falling over the old Singh Haveli. He could not have been older than eight. The estate looked very different then. Before expansion, before money, before politics, and before wars. Back then it was simply home. A large ancestral property surrounded by fields and mud roads. One evening he had climbed onto the rooftop during a storm. He wanted to see lightning. His father nearly beat him for it afterward. But before that happened, Vikram had found him. The memory felt so vivid that Vardaan could almost hear the rain again.

—Pagal ho gaya baa ka?

Vikram had shouted while climbing the stairs.

—Bijli gir jaayi toh?

"What if lightning strikes you?"

Young Vardaan laughed.

—Hum astronaut banab.

"I'm going to become an astronaut."

Vikram rolled his eyes.

—Tu pahile zinda ta rah.

"First survive."

The brothers sat beneath the rain for nearly an hour. Watching the sky. Watching the lightning. Watching the stars appear whenever the clouds briefly parted. That was the first time Vardaan spoke aloud about leaving. About studying. About space. About a life beyond the empire. Beyond the district. Beyond India itself. Most people laughed when he said such things. Vikram never did. Never.

The memory shifted. Years passed. The estate grew larger. The empire grew stronger. And Vardaan grew older. By then he understood what his family really was. The villagers called them protectors. The newspapers called them businessmen. The police called them influential. Their enemies called them criminals. The truth existed somewhere in the middle.

The Singh Empire employed thousands. Transport companies. Brick kilns. Coal routes. Construction projects. Warehouses. Agricultural lands. Everything generated money. Power. Influence. And enemies. Always enemies. As a teenager, Vardaan hated it. He hated the armed guards. The politicians visiting the house. The endless disputes. The fear. The whispers. The violence that followed the family everywhere. Vikram accepted it. Vardaan rejected it. That difference defined their lives.

The aircraft shook slightly. Turbulence.

Several passengers stirred. A flight attendant walked quietly through the aisle. Vardaan remained lost in thought. Another memory surfaced. This one is even darker. More painful. The night everything changed.

His father, Vairav Singh, stood in the main courtyard. Several men surrounded him. Politicians. Contractors. Party leaders. District officials. Everybody wanted something. Everybody needed something. Nobody ever left empty-handed. Vardaan remembered standing beside Vikram. Watching. Listening. Learning. His father looked invincible. Like one of those ancient kings described in mythology. A ruler who believed his kingdom would last forever. Then Bajwa arrived. Even now, the memory felt strange. Because when Vardaan thought about Bajwa, he remembered laughter. Not fear. Not hatred. Laughter. The man was family. Practically an uncle. A constant presence in their lives. Vairav and Bajwa were inseparable. At least that was what everyone believed. The empire itself had been built by both men. Together. Side by side. Two brothers against the world. Or so the story went.

Vardaan remembered Bajwa ruffling his hair that evening.

—Bada aadmi banba ka, Chhotka?

"Gonna become a big man?"

Before Vardaan could answer, Vikram replied.

—Ee bada aadmi na bani.

"He's not becoming a big man."

—Bada scientist bani.

"He'll become a scientist."

Everyone laughed. Even Vairav. Especially Vairav.The memory lingered painfully. Because none of them knew what was coming. None of them knew that one day those same relationships would become battle lines.

The aircraft cabin remained silent. Outside, dawn slowly emerged over distant clouds. A pale orange horizon appeared. Beautiful. Vardaan barely noticed. His thoughts had already returned to Vikram. Always Vikram.

The argument happened in 2001. The biggest fight of their lives. Vardaan had received admission offers from America. One of the best aerospace programs in the world. For him, it was a dream. For Vairav Singh, it was betrayal. The old man exploded.

—You are Singh! You have responsibilities! The empire needs successors!

For hours they argued. Neither side is willing to surrender. Finally Vairav issued an ultimatum. Stay. Or leave forever.

That night Vardaan packed his bags. He truly intended to leave. And never return. Then someone knocked on his door. Vikram. Of course it was Vikram. It was always Vikram. The elder brother entered quietly and sat beside him. For several minutes neither spoke. Then Vikram handed him an envelope. Plane tickets. Documents. Money. Everything needed for the journey. Vardaan stared at him.

—You arranged all this?

Vikram nodded.

—What about Bauji?

—Mein Sambhal lunga.

—Aur ye baaki saab kuchh?

—I'll handle that too.

—Aur tumhara kya ?

For the first time, Vikram looked away. A small smile appeared on his face. The kind of smile that hid pain.

—Somebody has to stay.

Those words haunted Vardaan for the next eighteen years. Because Vikram stayed. And Vardaan left. One inherited the stars. The other inherited the kingdom, and the curse with it. The seatbelt sign illuminated. The captain's voice echoed through the cabin. They were beginning their descent toward Dubai. Passengers slowly woke up. Windows opened. Phones appeared. Conversations resumed. The ordinary rhythms of life returned.

Vardaan remained silent. Because another realization had finally settled inside him. A painful one. He had spent eighteen years believing he escaped. Believing he had chosen freedom. Believing he had earned his new life. But perhaps that wasn't entirely true. Perhaps Vikram had given it to him. Purchased it. Protected it. Carried its cost. Every year. Every burden. Every threat. Every enemy. While Vardaan built rockets. Vikram built walls. Walls that kept darkness away from his younger brother. Now those walls are gone.

And for the first time since leaving India, Vardaan found himself asking a question he had avoided for nearly two decades. What exactly had Vikram died protecting? The answer waited on the other side of the world. Beyond the airport. Beyond the empire. And deep inside the ruins of a family that had spent generations mistaking power for destiny. The aircraft descended through the clouds. India was getting closer. So was the truth.

CHAPTER THREE

The Funeral of a King

Singh Haveli, Bihar-Jharkhand Border - February, 2019

The helicopter appeared before the estate did.

As Vardaan's SUV climbed the final stretch of road leading toward the Singh Haveli, the distant thumping of rotor blades echoed across the valley. Thup. Thup. Thup. The sound rolled over coal fields and brick kilns. Over rivers darkened by mining runoff. The entire region seemed frozen beneath a blanket of mourning.

Vardaan looked through the tinted window. The road ahead was packed. Thousands of people. Not hundreds. Thousands. Men. Women. Old farmers. Truck drivers. Coal workers. Contractors. Village elders. Political workers. Police personnel. Everywhere. As far as the eye could see. For a moment he thought there must have been some public rally. Then reality struck. They had come for Vikram. The realization hit harder than the news of his death. Because for eighteen years, Vardaan had deliberately distanced himself from everything associated with the Singh Empire. He knew it was powerful. He knew it was wealthy. He knew Vikram commanded influence. But influence was an abstract word. This was not. This was real. This was grief. A collective grief. People stood silently along the roads holding marigold garlands. Some cried openly. Some folded their hands toward the passing convoy. Others simply stared. The expression on their faces resembled something Vardaan had only seen during state funerals. As if a ruler had fallen.

Inside the vehicle, Ramdeen sat beside him. The old caretaker looked twenty years older than he had during their last meeting. His eyes were swollen. His shoulders bent. His voice carried the exhaustion of someone who had not slept in days.

—Dekhat bani na, Chhote Malik?

Vardaan nodded silently. Ramdeen looked outside.

—Ee sab log Vikram Baba ke laage aail ba.

All these people have come for Vikram. The old man's voice cracked.

—Jab se khabar phailal baa, log ghar na gayil.

Since the news spread, people haven't gone home. Vardaan remained silent. His throat felt tight. The convoy moved slowly through the crowd. Nobody shouted. Nobody pushed. Nobody created chaos. The silence itself felt overwhelming. A strange realization began forming inside him. Perhaps he never truly knew his brother. The Singh Haveli emerged from the haze like an ancient fortress. Massive stone walls. Watchtowers. Iron gates. Multiple courtyards. Dozens of security personnel. Luxury vehicles lined the entrance. Government SUVs. Police escorts. Political convoys. Media vans. The estate looked less like a family home and more like the headquarters of a small kingdom. As the gates opened, Vardaan noticed something unusual. Nobody checked the arriving vehicles. Nobody stopped anyone. The guards simply stepped aside. The usual discipline seemed absent. The estate itself felt wounded. Like a body missing its heart. The SUV rolled into the main courtyard. Then stopped. For several seconds Vardaan remained seated. Unable to move. Unable to prepare himself.

Ramdeen placed a trembling hand on his shoulder.

— Chali, Chhote Malik.

Come.

Vardaan nodded. The door opened. The moment he stepped outside, the noise vanished. Not because the crowd became quiet. Because his mind stopped hearing. Everything narrowed into a single image. At the center of the courtyard stood a raised platform draped in white cloth. Flowers surrounded it. Candles burned around it. Thousands watched it. And upon it rested Vikram Singh. For a moment Vardaan simply stared. Unable to accept what his eyes were seeing. The face looked familiar. Too familiar. Yet wrong. Still. Silent. Absent. The face of a man who should have been laughing. Arguing. Giving orders. Protecting everyone. Instead, he lay motionless beneath a mountain of flowers. The king was dead. And suddenly Vardaan could not breathe.

The crowd parted. Vardaan walked toward the platform. One step. Then another. Then another. Every step felt heavier than the last. Memories assaulted him. *"Vikram teaching him cricket". "Vikram helping him study". "Vikram defending him against their father". "Vikram driving him to the airport". "Vikram waving goodbye". "The last time they met". "The last time they hugged"*. The last time either brother knew it was the last time. His legs weakened. Yet he kept walking. Until finally he stood beside the body. Close enough to touch. Close enough to see every detail. The bullet wound had been concealed. The injuries hidden. The funeral preparations were perfect. But death always left traces. A strange stillness. A terrible absence. Vardaan slowly reached forward. His hand touched Vikram's forehead. Cold. The moment shattered him. For eighteen years he had imagined returning home one day. Perhaps for a wedding. Perhaps for a celebration. Perhaps for reconciliation. Never this. Never this. A tear escaped before he could stop it. Then another. Then another. And suddenly the scientist. The exile. The man who escaped. Disappeared. Only a younger brother remained. Grieving. Broken. Alone.

A voice interrupted the silence.

—Vardaan.

He turned. And found himself facing Bajwa. Time had changed the man. But not entirely. The same broad shoulders. The same sharp eyes. The same commanding presence. Only older. Harder. More difficult to read. Bajwa stepped forward and embraced him. For several seconds neither spoke. Then Bajwa said quietly,

—Hum tohra ke bulawe ke kabhu na chahat rahni.

I never wanted to call you back. Vardaan looked at him. Bajwa's eyes moved toward Vikram's body.

—Par ab zaroorat pad gayil baa.

But now it has become necessary. Something about the statement lingered. Not the words. The tone. As though Vikram's death was not merely a tragedy. But a problem. A crisis. A vacuum. Before Vardaan could respond, another voice emerged behind him. A woman's voice. Soft. Tired. Broken.

—Unnish Saal.

Vardaan turned. Nandini stood several feet away. Wearing white. Her face pale from grief. Eyes swollen from endless crying. For a moment he barely recognized her. Then memories returned. The schoolteacher. Vikram's love. Vikram's future. The woman he was supposed to marry within weeks. Now a widow before becoming a bride. Nandini looked at him. A faint smile appeared. Heartbreaking in its fragility.

—Unnish Saal, Vardaan.

He lowered his gaze.

—I know.

—No.

Her voice trembled.

—You don't.

The words struck harder than intended. Not cruel. Simply true. Vardaan was gone. While everyone else remained. While Vikram fought wars. Built alliances. Protected businesses. Managed crises. Loved people. Buried people. Lived. Vardaan had been looking at stars. Nandini wiped her eyes.

—Aisa ek din na gaya ho jis din woh tumhara baat nehi kiye ho.

The statement surprised him.

—Sacchi?

A sad laugh escaped her.

—Har roz. Chhote kehta tha yeh, chhote bolta tha yeh, chhote rehta toh yeh, sirf chhote chhote chhote.

She looked toward Vikram's body.

—He was proud of you.

For the first time since arriving, guilt overwhelmed grief. Because he had not called enough. Had not visited enough. Had not been present. The empire always felt distant. Until now.

Later that evening, after politicians delivered speeches and religious rituals concluded, Vardaan finally found a moment alone. He climbed to the rooftop of the old haveli. The same rooftop where he and Vikram once watched storms. The same rooftop where dreams were born. The estate stretched endlessly below. Lights glowed across the property. Security patrols moved through the darkness. Thousands still remained outside the gates. Refusing to leave. Mourning. Waiting. The scale of it all felt impossible. Then footsteps approached. Ramdeen. The old caretaker carried two cups of tea. Just like he used to. Years ago. Neither spoke immediately. They stood side by side overlooking the estate. Finally Vardaan asked the question that had haunted him since arriving.

—Kaun maara Vikram ko?

Who killed Vikram?

Ramdeen stared into the darkness. His expression changed. Fear. Real fear. The old man lowered his voice.

—Naam sab jaane la.

Everyone knows the name.

—Pratap Chauhan.

The name meant little to Vardaan. But the way Ramdeen spoke it did not. The old caretaker continued.

—Ab ee ilaka badal gayil baa, Malik.

This region has changed.

—Bahut log badal gayil baa.

Many people have changed. The wind swept across the rooftop. Carrying distant sounds from the crowd below. Ramdeen looked toward the horizon. Toward the darkness beyond the estate.

—Vikram Baba ke maut...

He paused.

—...bas ek hatya na rahal.

It wasn't just a murder.

Vardaan slowly turned. The old man's eyes remained fixed on the darkness.

—Itihas badal gayil baa.

History has changed.

Far away, somewhere beyond the coal fields and transport routes, thunder rolled across the night sky. The first storm clouds were gathering. And neither man yet understood that Vikram Singh's death was only the first move in a war decades in the making.

CHAPTER FOUR

The Kingdom Without A King

Singh Haveli , Three Days After Vikram's Funeral

Death leaves slowly. The funeral ends. The flowers dry. The mourners return home. The speeches stop. The rituals conclude. But grief remains. Lingering like smoke after a fire. Three days had passed since Vikram Singh's cremation. Yet the Haveli still felt occupied by his absence. Every corridor carried his memory. Every chair seemed to wait for him. Every employee instinctively looked toward places where he no longer stood. The Singh Empire had survived gang wars. Political coups. Mining disputes. Police crackdowns. Economic crashes. But nobody had prepared for this. Nobody had prepared for a future without Vikram. Especially Vardaan. For three days he barely left the estate. Not because anyone asked him to stay. Because he didn't know where else to go. America felt distant. Unreal. A previous Birth. The stars now seemed farther away than the villages surrounding the Haveli. And every passing hour brought a new visitor. Everyone arrived with the same expression. Condolences. And fear. A dangerous combination.

The first real meeting happened on the fourth morning. The old Durbar Hall had once hosted weddings. Political negotiations. Business deals. Even ceasefire agreements between rival factions. Now it hosted uncertainty. Vardaan entered quietly. The room immediately fell silent. More than thirty people sat around the enormous teakwood table. Many of them had known him since childhood. Yet they stared at him like a stranger. Which, in many ways, he was. At the far end sat Bajwa. Calm.Composed. Watching. The old lion of the Empire. Time had silvered his beard. But not diminished his authority. To Vardaan's surprise, Bajwa stood as soon as he entered. A gesture of respect. Or something else.

—Dekha sab?

Bajwa looked around the room.

—Ee Vardaan baa.

This is Vardaan.

Nobody spoke. Bajwa continued.

—Vikram ke chhota bhai. Vairav Singh ke beta.

"The son of Vairav Singh."

The room remained silent. Until finally an elderly transporter stood. His hands folded respectfully.

—Hamra ke malik na chahi.

"We don't need a ruler."

The statement confused Vardaan. The man continued.

—Hamra ke rakshak chahi.

"We need a protector."

Several others nodded. Vardaan suddenly understood. They weren't comparing him to Vairav. Or Bajwa. They were comparing him to Vikram. An impossible standard.

The meeting lasted six hours. And by its end, Vardaan's understanding of the Empire had changed completely. The Singh Empire wasn't merely a criminal organization. It was an ecosystem. Coal routes. Transport syndicates. Brick manufacturing. Land holdings. Warehousing. Construction contracts. Political alliances. Security operations. Legal businesses. Illegal businesses. Entire districts depended upon its stability. Thousands of families earned their livelihoods through Singh-controlled networks. If the Empire collapsed, entire communities would suffer. For the first time in his life, Vardaan understood why Vikram stayed. And why leaving had been so difficult for him. Because the Empire wasn't just power. It was responsibility. Heavy. Unrelenting. And dangerous.

Late that evening, Vardaan sat alone in Vikram's office. The room remained untouched. Nobody had moved anything. Not a single object. The large wooden desk still contained unfinished paperwork. A half-read book. Several handwritten notes. A family photograph. A cup of tea long gone cold. The office felt frozen in time. As though Vikram might return at any moment. Vardaan opened a drawer. Inside lay dozens of files. Business records. Contracts. Financial reports. Nothing unusual. Until one particular folder caught his attention. It was thinner than the others. Marked only with a single name. PRATAP. Nothing else. No surname. No title. Just: PRATAP.

Vardaan opened it. Empty. Every document had been removed. Every page is missing. Only a single photograph remained. An old photograph. Perhaps fifteen years old. The image showed Vikram standing beside a younger man. Both smiling. Both covered in coal dust. The younger man looked proud. Loyal. Almost brotherly. Vardaan turned the photograph over. On the back, written in Vikram's handwriting: *"Some bonds are stronger than blood."* A chill ran down his spine. Because the man in the photograph was Pratap Chauhan. The man who murdered Vikram.

That night sleep refused to come. Near midnight, Vardaan found himself wandering through the old sections of the Haveli. Most of the staff had retired. Only security personnel remained awake. The estate felt strangely alive in darkness. Ancient. Haunted. Eventually he reached a forgotten corridor near the western wing. A section rarely used anymore. The walls displayed old family photographs. Generations of Singh history. Vairav. Savitri. Young Vikram. Childhood images. Business inaugurations. Political ceremonies. Then he noticed something unusual. One photograph appeared damaged. Not by age. Deliberately. The frame remained intact. But someone's face had been scratched away. Violently. Repeatedly. Only fragments remained visible. A shoulder. Part of a hand. The outline of a jaw. Nothing more. Vardaan stepped closer. Something about the image felt familiar. Then he noticed the caption. His heartbeat slowed. The photograph had been taken nearly thirty years earlier. And the people identified beneath it were: *VAIRAV SINGH. BAJWA. SAVITRI.* The fourth name had been scratched out completely. Someone had wanted that person erased. Not forgotten. Erased.

Footsteps echoed behind him. Vardaan turned. Ramdeen stood at the end of the corridor. The old caretaker's expression changed immediately. Fear. The same fear he displayed on the rooftop.

—Ee photo ke ka dekhat bani?

"What are you doing looking at that photograph?"

Vardaan pointed.

—Woh Kaun hai?

Ramdeen remained silent.

—Kaun hai?

"Who was he?"

The old man's face tightened. For several seconds he said nothing. Then quietly:

—Kabhi-kabhi, Malik...

"Sometimes..."

—...purana sach maral rahe ta hi accha hola.

"...old truths are better left buried."

The answer only deepened the mystery.

Hours later, long after midnight, another man stood awake. Miles away. Far beyond the Singh estate. Far beyond the villages. Far beyond the coal belt. Inside an isolated farmhouse hidden among abandoned brick kilns. A single lamp illuminated the darkness. The room contained maps. Weapons. Photographs. Business records. Political contacts. Plans. Years of plans. The man sitting alone studied a photograph carefully. Vikram. Vardaan. The Singh family. His expression revealed nothing. No anger. No satisfaction. No regret. Only patience. The patience of someone who had waited a very long time. A younger associate entered the room.

—Naya malik laut aaya.

"The new heir has returned."

The man smiled faintly. Not because he was surprised. Because he had expected it. He always expected it. His eyes remained fixed upon Vardaan's photograph. Then he spoke for the first time. A calm voice. A dangerous voice. The voice of a man who already understood the board while everyone else was still learning the rules.

—Achha.

"Good."

The smile widened slightly.

—Ab khel shuru hoga.

"Now the game begins."

The lamp flickered.

And for the first time —The shadow of Pratap Chauhan entered the board.

CHAPTER FIVE

The Name That Refused To Die

Singh Haveli, February, 2019

The night refused to leave Vardaan alone. Even after returning to his room, sleep never arrived. The damaged photograph remained trapped inside his mind. Vairav Singh. Bajwa. Savitri. And the fourth man. The erased man. Someone had scratched away the face with such rage that even the frame carried scars. It wasn't vandalism. It was hatred. Personal hatred. The kind that survived decades. The kind that outlived death itself. Vardaan sat beside the window as dawn slowly emerged beyond the estate. Coal trucks were already moving across distant roads. Brick kiln chimneys released dark smoke into the sky. The Empire had begun another day. As though nothing had happened. As though Vikram had never died. As though kings could be replaced. His jaw tightened. That realization hurt most. The world always moves forward. Only memories remained behind.

The next morning brought visitors. Again. The stream of mourners had ended. Now came businessmen. Politicians. Police officers. Union leaders. Contractors. People who needed answers. People who feared uncertainty. And increasingly, people who feared one particular name. Pratap Chauhan. The name appeared everywhere. In whispers. In unfinished conversations. In nervous glances. Yet nobody spoke about him openly. Which only increased

Vardaan's curiosity. By noon he finally decided hc had heard enough. He summoned Ramdeen. The old caretaker arrived carrying tea. As always. As if some habits remained untouched by tragedy.

— Baithiye.

Ramdeen hesitated. Then sat. Vardaan wasted no time.

— Pratap Chauhan ke baare mein sab kuch bataiye.

Tell me everything about Pratap Chauhan.

The old man's expression darkened immediately. He looked toward the closed door. Then toward the windows. Then back at Vardaan.

— Ee naam bahut din baad sunat bani.

I am hearing this name after many days.

— Toh bataiye.

Ramdeen remained silent for several moments. Then slowly nodded.

— Thik baa.

"Fine."

The old man placed the tea tray aside. His eyes drifted toward the courtyard. Toward the place where Vikram's body had rested days earlier. And then he began.

— Pratap pahile dushman na rahal.

Pratap wasn't an enemy at first. The statement surprised Vardaan. Ramdeen continued.

— Woh Apna hi moora tha, Vikram Baba ka jigra dost.

The words landed heavily. Family. The same word is used in Vikram's photograph. The same word written on the back. "*Some bonds are stronger than blood.*" Suddenly the sentence felt far more dangerous. Ramdeen leaned back. Lost in memory.

— Karib bees saal pahile ke baat baa.

This was nearly twenty years ago.

— Tab Vikram Baba jawaan rahas, aapke jaane ka kuch saal baad.

Vikram was still young, after a few years you went away.

— Au sab kuchh tootat rahal.

And the empire was breaking apart.

The years following Vairav Singh's death had been brutal. Coal contracts disappeared. Transport routes were attacked. Politicians changed loyalties. Criminal gangs emerged from every direction. Everyone believed the Singh Empire would collapse. Then Pratap arrived. Not as a gangster. Not as a rival. But as a savior.

— Au Vikram Baba ka jaan bachail, woh bhi teen teen baar.

Ramdeen's voice carried genuine admiration.

— Teen baar.

Three times. The first time during a transport ambush. The second time during a political rally attack. The third time during a land dispute that turned into a gunfight. Each time Pratap stood beside Vikram. Each time he risked his own life, to save Vikram's. Each time he earned greater trust. Until eventually he became inseparable from the family.

— Log kahat rahas ki Vikram Baba ke do bhai baa.

People used to say Vikram had two brothers.

— Ek Vardaan.

— Ek Pratap.

The sentence struck Vardaan like a punch. Because he suddenly understood something. Pratap hadn't merely betrayed Vikram. He had betrayed a brother. Which meant the eventual murder was far worse than simple assassination. It was treason of the soul.

— Phir kya badal gayi?

Vardaan asked quietly.

Ramdeen's expression hardened.

— Hum na jaane.

I don't know.

The answer came too quickly. Too rehearsed. Vardaan noticed. Ramdeen noticed that Vardaan noticed. An uncomfortable silence followed. Finally the old caretaker sighed.

— Sab kuch badal gayil jab Bajwa sahib ke kuch purana log waapas ailan.

Everything changed when some of Bajwa's old associates returned. The statement seemed insignificant. Yet something about it lingered. Old associates. From where? Why now? Before Vardaan could ask further, a knock interrupted them.

A security guard entered hurriedly.

— Malik.

The young man looked nervous.

— Bahar kuch log aail baa.

Some men have come outside.

— Kaun?

—Coal union waale.

The guard hesitated.

— Pratap ke log ke dhamki milal baa.

They've received threats from Pratap's men. The room immediately grew tense. Ramdeen looked away. Vardaan stood. For the first time since arriving home, he felt something different from grief. Responsibility. And responsibility demanded action.

The meeting took place inside an old warehouse office near the transport yard. Nearly thirty workers waited anxiously. Most looked exhausted. Many carried visible injuries. Several trucks parked outside displayed bullet damage. The message was obvious. Someone was applying pressure. Aggressively. The moment Vardaan entered, the room fell silent. Every eye turned toward him. Not because they trusted him. Because they were judging him. Trying to determine whether the younger Singh possessed even a fraction of Vikram's strength. An elderly union leader stepped forward. His face carried decades of coal dust and hardship.

— Malik.

He folded his hands respectfully.

— Humni ke bachai.

Save us. The simplicity of the request unsettled Vardaan. In America, problems were solved through meetings. Research. Data. Procedure. Here people expected protection. Immediate protection. Physical protection. A completely different world. The union leader continued.

— Pratap ke log hafta maangta.

Pratap's men are demanding payments.

— Na di ta truck jala deta.

If we refuse, they burn the trucks. Another worker spoke.

— Kal raat hamaar bhai ke pitai kar delan.

Last night they beat my brother. Anger spread through the room. Fear followed. Vardaan listened carefully. For nearly an hour. Collecting information. Observing. Thinking. Exactly the way a scientist would. And slowly a realization emerged. Pratap wasn't simply attacking businesses. He was attacking confidence. Attacking faith. Attacking the idea that the Singhs could still protect anyone. Which meant this wasn't random violence. It was a strategy. A campaign. A systematic dismantling of authority. Someone intelligent was orchestrating it. Someone patient. Someone who understood power.

That evening Vardaan sat once again in Vikram's office. This time he wasn't grieving. He was studying. Maps covered the desk. Transport routes. Coal corridors. Political territories. Warehouse locations. Brick kiln networks. For hours he examined everything. Searching for patterns. Searching for weaknesses. Searching for Pratap. Then suddenly something clicked. A transport route. One specific route. Every recent attack had occurred near it. Every reported threat connected back to it. Every disruption originated from the same corridor. Vardaan stared at the map. The answer seemed almost obvious now.

— Interesting.

A voice emerged behind him. Vardaan turned. Bajwa stood in the doorway. Watching. Observing. The older man approached slowly. His eyes drifted toward the map. Then toward the marked route. A faint smile appeared.

— Tohra mein Vairav ke dimaag baa.

You have Vairav's mind. The compliment felt genuine. Yet somehow unsettling. Bajwa pointed toward the route.

— Pratap ee jagah ke peecha kyon padal baa, jaane la?

Know why he's obsessed with this area? Vardaan shook his head. Bajwa's expression darkened.

— kahe ki ehi se sabkuchh shuru bhail.

The answer immediately captured his attention. Bajwa continued.

— pahila int ke bhttha..

— pahila trak depo.

— pahila koyala ke theka.

Everything started there. The original foundation. The birthplace of the Singh Empire. Then the older man looked directly into Vardaan's eyes.

— Pratap power na todat baa.

Pratap isn't attacking the power.

— u itihas pe hmla kar rahal bade.

The words remained in the room long after Bajwa stopped speaking. Because deep down, Vardaan knew they were true.

Late that night, many miles away, another meeting unfolded. Inside an abandoned brick kiln complex hidden beyond the river. Dozens of armed men gathered around furnace fires. Weapons rested against walls. Motorcycles lined the courtyard. The atmosphere resembled a military camp more than a criminal hideout. At the center sat Pratap Chauhan. The first proper glimpse of the man whose shadow had haunted so far. He looked older than the photograph. Harder. Scarred. The face of someone shaped by violence. Yet his eyes remained intelligent. Patient. Dangerously patient. One of his lieutenants approached.

— Vardaan Singh active ho gayil baa.

Vardaan has become active. Pratap smiled. Not mockingly. Almost proudly. As if hearing news about a worthy opponent.

— Achha.

Good.

The lieutenant looked confused.

— Ee problem na baa?

Isn't that a problem? Pratap stared into the furnace flames. For several seconds he said nothing. Then finally spoke. A quiet voice. Measured. Thoughtful.

— Na.

"No." His eyes reflected the firelight.

— Problem tab hovat...

The problem would be...

—...jab Vikram zinda rahit.

...if Vikram were still alive.

Silence followed. Even his own men seemed uncomfortable. Because there was no hatred in his voice. Only sadness. A sadness that did not belong to ordinary enemies. Pratap slowly stood. His gaze moved toward the darkness beyond the kiln. Toward the direction of the Singh estate. Toward the future. Toward war. Then he spoke again. Almost to himself.

— Ab dekhat bani...

Now let's see...

—...Vardaan Singh apne bhai jaisan baa...

...whether Vardaan Singh is like his brother...

—...ya apne baap jaisan.

...or like his father.

The furnace roared. The flames climbed higher. And somewhere far away, inside the Singh Haveli, Vardaan unknowingly took his first step toward becoming the man destiny had always reserved for him.

CHAPTER SIX

THE LAND OF RED DUST

Bharat Brick Works, Bihar–Jharkhand Border, March, 2019

The earth itself seemed wounded. That was the first thought that entered Vardaan's mind. As the convoy moved deeper into Singh territory, the landscape slowly transformed. Green fields disappeared. Villages became sparse. The roads narrowed. And gradually the world turned red. Red dust. Red clay. Red earth. The very soil seemed stained with dried blood. Hundreds of trucks moved along broken roads carrying coal, bricks, stone and construction material. The air smelled of smoke. Diesel. Sweat. And something older. Something primitive. The smell of labor. The smell of survival. Vardaan lowered the SUV window slightly. Warm wind rushed inside. Along with dust. Ramdeen immediately frowned.

— Khidki band kari, Malik.

Close the window.

— Ee mitti kapra ke andar ghus jaala.

This dust enters everything. But Vardaan ignored him. For the first time since returning home, he wanted to see. Not reports. Not maps. Not numbers. Reality. The land Vikram died protecting.

The convoy eventually approached a massive industrial complex. Several brick kilns rose into the sky like ancient towers. Smoke drifted endlessly from their chimneys. Thousands of workers moved across the grounds. Men. Women. Teenagers. Families. Entire lives built around fire and clay. A rusted iron sign stood near the entrance. ***"BHARAT BRICK WORKS EST. 1982"*** The paint had faded. But the name remained. Bajwa's words echoed in Vardaan's mind. "The Empire was born here." The gates opened. Workers immediately noticed the arriving vehicles. Conversations stopped. Machines slowed. Faces turned. The younger Singh had arrived.

The manager greeted them nervously. His name was Jagdish Yadav. A short man with permanently coal-stained hands. He folded both palms.

— Pranam, Malik.

Vardaan nodded.

— Sab theek chal raha hai?

Jagdish laughed bitterly.

—Na, Malik.

At least he was honest. The manager guided them through the facility. Kilns. Storage yards. Loading zones. Coal stockpiles. Labor colonies. The scale surprised Vardaan. Thousands worked here. Thousands. One facility. One business. One little piece of the Empire. Suddenly he understood why Vikram never escaped. How could anyone abandon responsibility for so many people?

They reached the oldest kiln. A massive circular structure blackened by decades of smoke. The workers called it: ***"Bharat Furnace."*** The original kiln. The first kiln. The heart of everything. Its walls looked ancient. Scarred by time. Almost sacred. Several older workers immediately gathered around Vardaan. One elderly laborer stared at him carefully. Then unexpectedly smiled.

— Bilkul Vikram Malik jaisan aankh baa.

Same eyes as Vikram. The others nodded. The old man continued.

— Bas gussa kam baa.

Just less anger. Laughter spread among the workers. For the first time in days, Vardaan smiled. A genuine smile. Small. But real. The old laborer introduced himself. Mahendra. Sixty-eight years old. Working at Bharat Brick Works since its foundation. Long before Vikram. Long before Vardaan left India. Long before the Empire became powerful. As they walked together, Mahendra spoke endlessly. Stories. Memories. History. And slowly the saga of the Singh family began taking shape.

— Ee jagah pahile jungle rahal.

This place used to be a jungle. Mahendra pointed toward the surrounding land.

— Kauno sadak na.

No roads.

— Kauno kaam na.

No work.

— Kauno rozi-roti na.

No livelihood. Then came Vairav Singh. And Bajwa. Together. The names immediately caught Vardaan's attention. Mahendra smiled nostalgically.

— Dono bhai jaisan rahas."

They were like brothers.

— Do badan par Ek jaan.

One soul. One life. The description sounded strangely familiar. Exactly how Ramdeen described Vikram and Pratap. The parallel lingered in Vardaan's mind. Mahendra continued.

— daku se ladt rahle.

— gaav ke raksa krt rahle.

— pahila bhttha apna hath se bnvle.

The old laborer touched the furnace wall gently. Almost reverently.

— Ee deewar par Vairav ke khoon lagal baa.

Vairav's blood is on these walls. The statement startled everyone.

— Khoon?

Blood? Mahendra nodded.

— Construction ke time accident bhayil rahal.

There had been an accident during construction. Vairav was injured. His blood stained the clay. The workers refused to remove it. They considered it a blessing. A foundation sacrifice. The story sounded almost mythical. Yet in places like these, myths and history often became inseparable.

Then Mahendra's expression changed. The smile faded. His eyes darkened.

— Ab sab badal gayil baa.

Everything has changed now. The atmosphere immediately shifted. Nobody laughed anymore. Nobody spoke. Several workers looked away. Vardaan noticed.

— What changed?

Mahendra hesitated. Then quietly replied.

— Pratap.

The name landed heavily. Like a stone dropped into still water. Even the wind seemed to pause. The old laborer lowered his voice.

— Ee jagah par pahile Vikram Malik aawat rahas.

Vikram used to come here regularly. Every month. Sometimes every week. He knew workers by name. Attended weddings. Paid hospital bills. Settled disputes. Protected families. The workers respected him. Not because he was powerful. Because he cared. Then Pratap arrived. And everything changed.

— Kaise?

How? Mahendra looked around carefully. Making sure nobody unfamiliar stood nearby. Then answered.

— Pratap bhi pahile accha rahal.

Pratap was good once too. That sentence surprised Vardaan more than anything. Again. The same pattern. Nobody described Pratap as a monster. Nobody described him as evil. Only changed. Something happened. Something transformed him. But what?

Later that afternoon the answer nearly arrived. Or at least part of it. While inspecting the loading yard, Vardaan noticed a damaged wall. Fresh bullet marks. Dozens of them. The concrete resembled a battlefield. Jagdish quickly tried changing the subject. Too quickly.

— Yeh kab hua?

Vardaan asked. The manager hesitated. Ramdeen immediately became uncomfortable. Nobody answered.

— Main pooch raha hoon.

His voice hardened.

— When?

Finally Jagdish sighed.

— Do hafte pehle.

Two weeks ago. Before Vikram's death. Several armed men had attacked the facility. No robbery. No theft. No kidnapping. Nothing. They simply fired upon the kiln. Destroyed equipment. Then left. A warning. Nothing more.

— Pratap?

Vardaan asked. Jagdish nodded. The manager's hands trembled slightly.

— Message bheja tha.

He had sent a message.

— What message?

The manager looked toward Bharat Furnace. Then quietly replied:

— Agla number itihaas ka hai.

History is next. The words sent a chill through Vardaan. Because Bajwa had said something similar. Pratap wasn't attacking businesses. He was attacking history.

The return journey began after sunset. Darkness covered the roads. Coal trucks formed endless lines across the highways. The convoy moved slowly through the night. Vardaan sat silently. Thinking. Analyzing. Connecting fragments. A scientist examining data. A strategist examining a battlefield. Something didn't fit. Pratap wanted history destroyed. Why? If his objective was power, there were easier targets. More profitable targets. More strategic targets. Yet every attack focused on symbols. Places. Memories. Foundations. The birthplace of the Empire. Almost as though he hated what the Empire represented. Not merely what it possessed. The realization disturbed him. Because hatred like that was personal. Very personal.

Around midnight the convoy stopped unexpectedly. The lead vehicle reported road damage ahead. Drivers exited. Security personnel spread out. The atmosphere immediately became tense. Too tense. Vardaan stepped outside. The highway felt unnaturally quiet. Then he saw it. A single object lying in the center of the road. Wrapped in cloth. Waiting. Like a gift. Or a threat. One guard approached cautiously. Unwrapped it. Everyone froze. Inside lay an old photograph. Nothing else. No letter. No message. Just a photograph. Vardaan took it. And felt his stomach tighten. The image showed four men standing beside the original Bharat Furnace decades earlier. Young. Smiling. Victorious. Vairav Singh. Bajwa. An unidentified worker. And—Pratap. Young. Barely twenty. Standing beside them. Like family. Like a son. Like an heir. On the back someone had written a single sentence. In red ink. *"Ask Bajwa what really happened"*.

The night suddenly felt colder. Far colder. For several seconds nobody spoke. Nobody moved. Then Ramdeen whispered:

— Hey Bhagwan...

My God. Vardaan stared at the photograph. The words. The faces. The implication. And for the first time since returning home— A dangerous thought entered his mind. Maybe he didn't know the whole story. Maybe nobody did. Far away, hidden somewhere beyond the darkness, a motorcycle engine started. A lone rider watched the convoy from a distant ridge. Watching. Waiting. Observing. Then disappearing into the night. The message had been delivered. The first crack had appeared. And somewhere deep within the foundations of the Singh Empire— Old ghosts had begun to wake.

CHAPTER SEVEN

The Woman Who Asked Questions

Singh Haveli, March, 2019

The photograph remained on Vardaan's desk all night. He must have looked at it fifty times. Perhaps more. Every time he studied it, a different detail emerged. A different question. A different mystery. The image had clearly been taken at Bharat Brick Works. Years ago. Long before Vikram became king. Long before Vardaan left for America. Long before the empire fractured. Four men stood together. Vairav Singh. Bajwa. Pratap. And another worker. All smiling. All looking toward the future. Nobody appeared afraid. Nobody appeared betrayed. Nobody appeared destined to kill each other. Yet somehow they had arrived there. The back of the photograph bothered him even more. Ask Bajwa what really happened. Not: Ask Bajwa who killed Vikram. Not: Ask Bajwa where Pratap is. Not: Ask Bajwa why there is war. Instead: Ask Bajwa what really happened. The wording suggested history. Something older. Something deeper. Something buried. Vardaan stared through the window. The first rays of sunlight touched the distant coal fields. Another day had begun. And with it, another lie. Or perhaps another truth. He no longer knew which.

By noon, Bajwa arrived. As he often did. Without announcement. Without ceremony. Walking through the Haveli as though it still belonged equally to him. Perhaps it did. In many ways, Bajwa had helped build every stone of it. The old man entered Vikram's office carrying tea.

— Abhi bhi kaagaz dekh raha baa?

Still studying papers?

Vardaan smiled faintly.

— Space research se aasaan baa.

Easier than space research. For the first time in days, Bajwa laughed. A genuine laugh. Warm. Almost fatherly. The sound felt strangely comforting. Which made what happened next even more uncomfortable. Without warning, Vardaan placed the photograph on the desk. Between them. Silence followed.

For the first time since Vardaan returned home, Bajwa's smile disappeared. Not entirely. Just enough. A small change. A crack. But Vardaan noticed. Scientists survived by noticing small changes.

— Kaun bhejal ee?

Who sent this? Bajwa asked quietly.

— I don't know.

The older man picked up the photograph. Studied it. His eyes lingered on Vairav. Longer than the others. Much longer. For several seconds he said nothing. Then slowly sat down.

— Tani purana tasveer baa.

A very old picture.

— Pratap ke pehchaanat bani?

Do you recognize Pratap?

Vardaan nodded.

— sabhe okra ke chinhat ba.

The answer drew another faint smile. This one is sadder. Older.

— oo hmesha i aadmi na rahle.

There it was again. The same sentence. Repeated by everyone. Workers. Ramdeen. Union leaders. Now Bajwa. Nobody described Pratap as evil. Only changed. The pattern was becoming impossible to ignore.

Bajwa placed the photograph down. Then looked directly at Vardaan.

— Tohra sach mein jaana baa?

Do you truly want to know?

— Haan.

The answer came immediately. Bajwa sighed. For a moment he seemed older than ever. As though carrying memories heavier than coal.

— Pratap anath rahal.

Pratap was an orphan. The revelation surprised Vardaan.

— bhttha ke aspas palal bdhal.

— trak yard ke aspas ke ba.

— mjdurn ke aspas.

— hamni ke bich.

The old man's voice softened.

— Hum log uske beta jaisan paalni.

We raised him like a son.

A chill moved through Vardaan. A son. Not an employee. Not a gangster. A son. Suddenly the future betrayal became even darker. Bajwa continued.

— u vairav ke puja kile.

— u vikram ke bhi puja kile.

— u hamni men se ago bne ke chaht rahle.

The old man stopped speaking. His eyes drifted toward the photograph. Toward the younger version of himself. Toward a time before everything broke.

— Phir Kaa bhail ba?

Vardaan asked. The room fell silent. Bajwa's expression changed. Closed. Guarded. A door slamming shut.

— kuchh kahani ke dafan chhod dihal i behtr ba.

Exactly the same answer Ramdeen had given. Word for word. Vardaan noticed immediately. So did Bajwa. For several seconds neither man spoke. Then the older man stood. Conversation over. Question unanswered. The mystery deepened.

That evening a new visitor arrived. And with her, another complication. Her name was Aarohi Sharma. Investigative journalist. Almost Thirty years old. Patna-born. Delhi-educated. Known for exposing corruption. Known for surviving threats.

Known for asking questions powerful men disliked. The security guards tried stopping her. She ignored them. Ramdeen tried delaying her. She ignored him too. Eventually she walked directly into Vikram's office. Without permission. Without hesitation. Without fear. Vardaan looked up from the desk. Immediately annoyed. Immediately curious. She wore simple clothes. No jewelry. No display of status. Only confidence. The dangerous kind. The kind that couldn't be bought.

— Mr. Singh.

Her tone remained professional.

— I'm sorry for your loss.

The words felt sincere. Unlike the politicians. Unlike the businessmen. Unlike everyone else.

— Thank you.

Vardaan said, Aarohi nodded. Then immediately opened her notebook. Business. No wasted time.

— Now I'd like to discuss your brother's murder.

Vardaan almost laughed. Everyone else avoided the subject. This woman attacked it head-on.

— You're too damn swift.

— I don't have the luxury of working slowly.

Fair answer. Very fair.

The interview lasted nearly two hours. Though it felt more like an interrogation. Aarohi asked about: *Vikram. The Empire. Pratap. Coal contracts. Transport routes. Political alliances. Old rivalries. Recent threats.* Everything. Nothing escaped scrutiny. By the end, Vardaan found himself oddly impressed. Because unlike everyone else, she wasn't afraid. Not of the Empire. Not of Pratap. Not of Bajwa. Not of anyone. Which meant she was either courageous. Or foolishly reckless. Perhaps both. Eventually she closed her notebook. One final question remained.

— The official story says Pratap killed Vikram.

— Yes.

She studied him carefully.

— Do you believe official stories?

The question lingered. Because Vardaan suddenly realized he didn't. Not anymore.

Later that night Aarohi drove back toward Patna. Alone. The highway is nearly empty. Her recorder rested on the passenger seat. Filled with notes. Questions. Contradictions. Enough material for several articles. Yet none of it interested her most. One detail kept repeating in her mind. Pratap. Always Pratap. Because years earlier she had heard the name before. Long before Vikram's murder. Long before the national media cared. Long before anyone paid attention. A memory surfaced. A file. An old investigation. One she never completed. Her hands tightened around the steering wheel. Because something about this story felt familiar. Dangerously familiar.

Meanwhile, sixty kilometers away, inside an abandoned railway warehouse, Pratap Chauhan sat alone. Rain hammered the tin roof. Thunder echoed through the darkness. A lantern burned beside him. On the table lay dozens of photographs. Vikram. Bajwa. Vairav. Workers. Political leaders. Police officers. The entire history of the Empire. Pinned. Catalogued. Studied. Like evidence. One lieutenant entered nervously.

— Malik.

Pratap looked up.

— foto unka lago pahunch gail."

A small smile appeared.

— Accha.

The lieutenant hesitated.

— hamni ke ab okra ke mar sakeni.

Silence. Then Pratap laughed. Not loudly. Not mockingly. Simply amused.

— okra ke mar din??

The man nodded. Pratap slowly stood. Walked toward the window. Looked out at the rain. For several moments he said nothing. Then quietly replied:

— Vardaan ke maar ke ka fayda?

What's the benefit of killing Vardaan? The lieutenant frowned.

— par oo to singh hyuven.

Pratap nodded.

— Ekdm, singh hyuven.

He turned. The lantern light revealed scars across his face. Old scars. Painful scars. Scars that carried history.

— mari aadmi shahid ho jala.

His voice remained calm. Measured. Dangerously intelligent.

— bakir zinda mard...

He paused. Looking toward a photograph of Bajwa.

—...zinda mard swal puchhela.

Thunder exploded outside. Pratap's eyes never left the photograph.

— aa swaln se shk paida ho jala, aa shk samrajyan ke tbah kar dela.

The warehouse fell silent. No one spoke. Because for the first time, even his own men understood something unsettling. Pratap Chauhan wasn't fighting for territory. Wasn't fighting for money. Wasn't fighting for power. He was fighting for the truth. And truths were far more dangerous than bullets.

Near midnight, while reviewing Vikram's old files, Vardaan discovered an envelope hidden behind a bookshelf. No label. No markings. No explanation. Inside lay a single piece of paper. Nothing else. Only one handwritten sentence. Written in Vikram's unmistakable handwriting. "*If anything happens to me...don't trust the story*". Vardaan stared at the words. Once. Twice. Three times. His heartbeat quickened. Outside, thunder rolled across the distant coal fields. Inside the room, silence thickened. Because for the first time— The dead had spoken. And what Vikram left behind wasn't an answer. It was a warning. The game had changed. And somewhere beyond the darkness, old ghosts were beginning to move.

CHAPTER EIGHT

The Dead Man's Warning

Singh Haveli, April, 2019

Rain continued throughout the night. Heavy. Relentless. As if the sky itself was attempting to wash away decades of blood. Vardaan sat alone in Vikram's office. The envelope remained open on the desk. The single sheet of paper lay before him. The handwriting was unmistakable. Vikram Singh. His brother. His protector. His hero. His last remaining family. And the message consisted of only six words. *If anything happens to me... don't trust the story.* Nothing else. No explanation. No names. No clues. No directions. Just a warning. A warning left by a man who knew death was approaching. Vardaan read it again. Then again. And again. The more he read it, the less he understood. What story? The official story? The police story? The media story? The story about Pratap? Or something much older? Something that had begun long before Vikram's murder? The office suddenly felt smaller. The walls seemed closer. The silence is heavier. For the first time since returning to India, Vardaan realized a frightening possibility. Perhaps Vikram's death was not the beginning of this story. Perhaps it was merely the latest chapter.

The next morning began with another surprise. Aarohi Sharma returned. This time she arrived carrying three old newspaper files. Several photographs. And a laptop. No condolences. No greetings.

No formalities. She entered the office and immediately dropped everything onto Vikram's desk.

— You're being lied to.

Vardaan looked up. That was quite an opening. Aarohi folded her arms.

— And deep down, I think you already know it.

The scientist inside him appreciated directness. The younger brother inside him hated it.

— What exactly are you talking about?

Instead of answering, Aarohi opened one of the files. Yellowed newspaper clippings spilled across the desk. Articles dating back nearly twenty years. Coal disputes. Transport wars. Political violence. Labor unrest. Names. Photographs. Records. Most were ordinary. One was not. A photograph. A younger Vikram. A younger Bajwa. And standing beside them— Pratap Chauhan. Not as an enemy. But as a guest of honor. At a Singh Foundation school inauguration. The photograph stunned him. Again. Another image. Another piece of evidence. Another contradiction. Aarohi watched his reaction carefully.

— You see the problem?

Vardaan nodded slowly. Pratap appeared everywhere. Everywhere. Not outside the family. Inside it, when he was away, busy chasing stars. For nearly two hours Aarohi explained her findings. Years earlier she had been investigating illegal mining operations across Bihar and Jharkhand. During that investigation one name kept appearing. Pratap Chauhan. But not as a criminal. As a problem-solver. Mediator. Negotiator. Protector. People respected him. Workers trusted him. Village leaders praised him. The records painted a very different picture from the monster everyone now described.

— Then what happened?

Vardaan asked. Aarohi shook her head.

— That's exactly what I've been trying to discover.

For years she had searched for the answer. And every trail ended the same way. Witnesses disappeared. Records vanished. People refused to talk. Almost as though someone wanted that chapter erased. The same way someone erased the face in the photograph. The same way Bajwa avoided questions. The same way Ramdeen avoided questions. A pattern was emerging. And patterns never lied.

By afternoon another lead appeared. Unexpectedly. Ramdeen. The old caretaker entered quietly carrying tea. Then noticed Aarohi. Immediately his expression darkened. Suspicion. Discomfort. Fear. Aarohi noticed. Of course she did. Journalists survived by noticing things, and anticipating changes.

— Ramdeen ji.

She smiled politely. The old man remained cautious.

— Ji.

— Aap Pratap ko toh acche se jaante honge, nehi?"

The question landed like a gunshot. Silence filled the room. Ramdeen's hands visibly tightened. The tea tray rattled slightly. Tiny movement. Huge revelation. Vardaan saw it. Aarohi saw it. Everyone saw it. For several seconds nobody spoke. Then Ramdeen placed the tray down. Very carefully. Very deliberately. And answered.

— Haan.

Yes. The word barely emerged. A whisper. A confession. A memory.

— Hum jaant rahe.

I knew him. The room became still. Even the ceiling fan seemed louder. Aarohi leaned forward.

— oo kaisa aadmi rahel?"

Ramdeen closed his eyes. And for a brief moment looked twenty years older.

— Bahut accha.

Very good. The answer came immediately. Without hesitation. Without calculation. Without fear. The truth. Perhaps the first honest truth anyone had spoken about Pratap.

— u bujurgo ke ijjat krela.

— majduron ke madad bhi krela.

— u bacchon ke rakccha krela.

— u vikram baba ko puja kile.

Ramdeen's voice trembled.

— Hum soch bhi na sakat rahni ki ek din...

I could never imagine that one day...The sentence died unfinished. Because even now he couldn't accept it. Couldn't reconcile memory with reality. Couldn't reconcile the brother with the murderer.

That evening Vardaan decided to visit the old labor colonies surrounding Bharat Brick Works. Without security. Without publicity. Without ceremony. Just observation. Just listening. The way a scientist conducted field research. The way Vikram apparently once had. Aarohi insisted on accompanying him. Against his better judgment. Against Ramdeen's advice. Against common sense. And so, shortly before sunset, they entered one of the oldest worker settlements in the region. The reaction surprised Vardaan.Children recognized the Singh name immediately. Elderly workers remembered Vairav. Women remembered Vikram. Stories emerged everywhere. Stories of hospital bills paid. School fees covered. Disputes settled. Families rescued. The Empire wasn't viewed as an organization. It was viewed as a family. A flawed family. But family nonetheless. Then someone mentioned Pratap. And once again the atmosphere changed. An elderly widow sitting outside her house looked toward the horizon. Toward the kilns. Toward the past. Then quietly said:

— Pratap beta bhi aisan hi rahal.

Pratap was the same. The same. Again. The same word. The same contradiction. The same impossible puzzle. Vardaan exchanged a glance with Aarohi. Both understood. The official story continued collapsing. Piece by piece.

Darkness had fallen by the time they returned. The roads were nearly empty. The air smelled of coal smoke and approaching rain. Halfway home, Vardaan noticed headlights behind them. One motorcycle. Maintaining distance. Following. Aarohi noticed too. Vardaan asked her,

— Friend of yours?

— No.

The motorcycle remained behind them for nearly ten kilometers. Never overtaking. Never retreating. Just watching. Observing. Then suddenly it accelerated. Passed them. And disappeared ahead. Gone. As quickly as it appeared. For several moments neither spoke. Then Aarohi pointed toward the road. A package lay in the center lane. Waiting. Just like before. The motorcycle had dropped it.

Inside the package they found a cassette tape. Old. Dusty. Unmarked. No explanation. No note. Nothing. Only the tape. Vardaan stared at it. Aarohi stared at it. Neither spoke. Because both already knew. This wasn't random. Someone wanted them to find it. Someone wanted them to hear it. The question was why.

They played the tape after midnight. Inside Vikram's office. Alone. The recording quality was poor. Crackling. Distorted. Ancient. For several seconds only static emerged. Then voices. Male voices. Arguing. Yelling. Threatening. And suddenly— Everyone froze. Because one of the voices belonged to Vairav Singh. Vardaan recognized it immediately from old recordings. His father. Dead for decades. Speaking from the grave. The tape continued. Fragments. Broken sentences. Unclear accusations. Then another voice emerged. A second man. Familiar. Painfully familiar. Bajwa. The room fell silent. Neither Vardaan nor Aarohi moved. The recording continued. Several words remained inaudible. Lost to time. Lost to damage. Then one sentence emerged clearly. Perfectly. Terrifyingly. Vairav's voice. Angry. Heartbroken. Betrayed.

— Tu humra bhai rahla...

You were my brother...A pause. Static. Then:

—...kahe kiyal re ee sab?

Why did you do all this? The tape abruptly ended. Silence. Nothing. No explanation. No conclusion. Only darkness. Only questions. Only dread. Aarohi slowly looked at Vardaan. Vardaan looked at the dead machine. Neither needed to speak. The implication was obvious. For years everyone believed the tragedy began with Pratap. But perhaps it didn't. Perhaps the wound existed much earlier. Perhaps the poison entered the family long before Vikram. Long before Vardaan. Long before Pratap.

Far away, inside a deserted railway warehouse, Pratap Chauhan sat alone. A single lantern illuminated the room. One of his men approached cautiously.

— Ta he tape mil gayil.

They found the tape. Pratap nodded. No surprise. No satisfaction. Only inevitability. As though events were unfolding exactly as planned. The lieutenant hesitated.

— Ab?

What now? Pratap stared at a photograph of Vikram. The same photograph he had studied countless times. His expression remained unreadable. Then quietly replied:

— Ab sach apna raasta khud banayega.

Now the truth will make its own path. Outside, thunder rolled across the coal belt. Inside, the lantern flame flickered. Miles away there is one small lingering fire of doubt that catches Vardaan's mind just enough to make Vardaan ask the one question that would eventually destroy everything. "*Who betrayed whom first?*"

CHAPTER NINE

THE KING'S FIRST WAR

Singh Haveli, April, 2019

Empires did not collapse in a day. They died piece by piece. Route by route. Contract by contract. Man by man. Vardaan learned this on a Tuesday morning. The news arrived shortly before sunrise. A convoy carrying coal from the Singh-controlled mines near Dhanbad had disappeared. Not one truck. Not two. Twelve. Twelve loaded trucks. Nearly three crores worth of material. Gone. Along with their drivers. And three contractors. The message was obvious. Someone had challenged the throne.

The emergency meeting began within an hour. The old Durbar Hall filled rapidly. Transport heads. Mining supervisors. Contractors. Political coordinators. Security chiefs. Everyone looked tense. Everyone looked afraid. At the center of the table sat Vardaan. For the first time, nobody looked toward Jay Singh Bajwa. Nobody looked toward Ramdeen. Nobody looked toward anyone else. They looked toward him. The room waited. The kingdom waited. The new king waited. A transport contractor stood first. Raghunath Singh. One of Vikram's oldest associates. His face carried bruises. One arm rested in a sling. His voice trembled with anger.

— Malik.

He folded his hands.

— Ee log had paar kar delan.

These people have crossed the line. The room erupted immediately. Several men shouted simultaneously.

— Truck jala det ba.

"They are burning our trucks."

— Hamaar log utha le jaata.

"They are kidnapping our men."

— Police bhi sunat na.

"The police aren't listening anymore."

Fear. Anger. Uncertainty. The same emotions that destroy empires. Vardaan listened quietly. Just as he had done inside research laboratories. Observation before action. Data before conclusion. Emotion never solves equations. Neither did panic. Eventually the room fell silent. Everyone waited. Then Vardaan spoke. Only one sentence.

— Last attack kab bhayil?

When was the last attack?

The question surprised everyone. Raghunath answered.

— Kal raat.

Last night. Vardaan nodded. Then asked another.

— Kahan par?

A map was immediately placed before him. He studied it. Five attacks. Six weeks. Different targets. Different routes. Different districts. Yet a pattern existed. He could see it. Others could not.

An hour later, after the meeting ended, Vardaan locked himself inside Vikram's office. Maps covered the walls. Attack reports. Route schedules. Transport records. Communication logs. A scientist's war room. Aarohi entered quietly. She stared at the chaos.

— Planning revenge?

Vardaan never looked up.

— No.

— Then?

He placed several photographs on the desk. Different attack sites. Different dates. Different locations. Aarohi studied them. For several moments she saw nothing. Then suddenly— She noticed. Every attack formed a rough circle. Around one specific location. One forgotten transport corridor. One abandoned loading depot.

— Someone is herding you.

She said quietly. Vardaan smiled. For the first time that day.

— Exactly.

Whoever orchestrated these attacks wanted Singh forces concentrated elsewhere. Meaning something valuable existed at the center. Something important. Something worth distracting them from.

By evening, Vardaan had his answer. The abandoned depot. Officially closed. Officially worthless. Unofficially? A major transit hub connecting three coal districts. If captured, it could cripple the Empire's logistics network. The trap became obvious. Which meant the response needed to be unexpected. Vardaan summoned the security chiefs. Twenty men entered. Most older than him. Most veterans. All killers. The kind of men who had fought beside Vairav, beside Vikram. Their expressions carried doubt. Not disrespect. Doubt. A scientist commanding soldiers. An unusual sight. Vardaan looked around the room. Then spoke calmly.

— Koi Badi gaari nahi.

The men exchanged confused glances. One finally spoke.

— Malik?

Vardaan pointed at the map.

"Hum truck na bhejab."

We won't send trucks. Silence. The security chief frowned.

— Phir?

Vardaan's eyes hardened. A little smile appeared on his lips, and said nothing.

The operation began at midnight. No official vehicles. No company markings. No large force. Only twelve SUVs. Forty armed men. And Vardaan himself. The convoy moved through darkness. Across broken roads. Past sleeping villages. Toward the abandoned depot. Nobody spoke much. Even the veterans seemed uncertain. Because nobody knew exactly what Vardaan intended. Only

Vardaan did.

The depot appeared shortly after two in the morning. Large. Isolated. Perfect for an ambush. Perfect for a takeover. The gates appeared abandoned. But appearances meant nothing. Vardaan knew that now. He studied the grounds through binoculars. Three lookout positions. Two hidden vehicles. Armed movement near the warehouses. Exactly as expected. The trap existed. Now it was time to spring it. One security chief leaned closer.

— Order, Malik?

The title still sounded strange. Yet somehow appropriate. Vardaan lowered the binoculars. Then quietly replied.

— Intezaar.

The men exchanged glances.

— Intezaar?

That was the order? Five minutes passed. Ten. Fifteen. Then suddenly — Three trucks approached from the northern road. Unmarked. Moving slowly. Exactly on schedule. The bait. The real target. Vardaan smiled. There it was. The final piece. The entire operation had been designed around those trucks. Not the Singh convoy. Not revenge. The trucks. The moment they entered the depot — Everything happened at once. Armed men emerged from hiding. Barricades appeared. Vehicles blocked exits. The depot transformed into a fortress. Vardaan stood.

— Ab.

The attack lasted less than seven minutes. Later, people would describe it differently. Some called it a battle. Others called it an execution. The truth existed somewhere in between. The Singh forces struck from three directions simultaneously. Precise. Disciplined. Overwhelming. Within minutes the depot belonged to them. The attackers surrendered. Or fled. The trucks remained intact. The cargo was secured. The operation finished. Clean. Efficient. Brutal. Exactly how Vikram would have wanted it. Or perhaps not. Even Vardaan wasn't sure anymore.

The real prize waited inside the lead truck. Not coal. Not weapons. Cash. Stacks upon stacks of cash. Enough to fund an army.

Enough to purchase politicians. Enough to start a war. The room fell silent. Even veteran gangsters looked shocked. One security chief whispered:

— Ee paisa kahaan jaa raha rahal?

Where was this money going? Nobody answered. Because everyone already knew. Pratap.

Among the captured men stood a regional lieutenant. One of Pratap's trusted operators. His name was Baleshwar. A feared figure throughout the transport network. For years he had terrorized contractors. Extorted businesses. Attacked drivers. Today he stood handcuffed. Defeated. Bleeding. Humiliated. The security chiefs looked toward Vardaan. Waiting. The old rules demanded blood. A public example. A message. The underworld understood only the consequences. Vardaan approached slowly. Baleshwar spat at his feet. A mistake. A very serious mistake. The warehouse fell silent. Everyone watched. The old empire. The new king. History waiting to choose a direction. For several seconds Vardaan said nothing. Then calmly crouched before him.

— Ek baat yaad rakha.

Remember one thing. His voice remained soft. Dangerously soft.

— Hum Vikram na bani.

I am not Vikram. Baleshwar laughed. Then Vardaan continued.

— Au hum Pratap bhi na bani.

And I am not Pratap. The smile from Baleshwar's face vanished. Vardaan stood, looking around the warehouse. Then issued an order.

— Release him.

The room froze. Even Aarohi, who had arrived later with local media contacts, looked stunned. Release him? Why? Vardaan answered the question before anyone asked.

— Jaa.

Go. Baleshwar stared in disbelief. Vardaan pointed toward the exit.

— Vairav Singh ke naam par empire khada bhayil."

The Empire was built alongside Vairav Singh.

— Jay Singh Bajwa uske badhaval."

Bajwa expanded it.

— Vikram Singh uske bachaval."

Vikram protected it. Then his eyes hardened. Ice cold.

— Ab hum chalawat bani."

Now I rule it. Silence consumed the warehouse. Even the air felt heavier. Baleshwar slowly backed away. Fear replacing arrogance. Vardaan took one final step forward. And delivered the message that would travel across the entire coal belt before sunrise.

— Pratap ke bol.

Tell Pratap.

— Singh Raj abhi khatam na bhayil baa.

Singh's rule has not ended.

— Bas naya raja baithal baa.

Only a new king sits on the throne.

The story spread rapidly. Across mines. Across transport routes. Across villages. Across political offices. Across police stations. Across the underworld. A single message. The scientist had entered the game. And he had won.

That night, inside a distant warehouse, Pratap Chauhan received the report.

He listened quietly. Without interruption. Without visible emotion. Then finally asked:

— Khud aail rahal?

He came himself?

The messenger nodded. Pratap smiled faintly. Not anger. Not hatred. Something else. Something closer to recognition. Then he looked toward Vikram's old photograph. The same photograph he always kept nearby. And for the first time in many years — He seemed worried. Because Vardaan Singh had finally stepped onto the battlefield. And the war had officially begun.

CHAPTER TEN

THE FIRST BLOOD

Dhanbad Coal Belt, May, 2019

By the first week of May, everyone understood one thing. The war had begun. Not officially. Not publicly. But across the coal belt, the signs were impossible to ignore. Trucks disappeared. Contracts collapsed. Supply routes shifted overnight. Politicians suddenly changed loyalties. Police officers stopped answering calls. Village strongmen began choosing sides. Every tea stall. Every transport office. Every coal depot. Every liquor shop. The same discussion echoed through the region.

— Pratap jeetat baa?

Is Pratap winning?

Or—

— Singh Raj lautat baa?

Is Singh Rule returning? Nobody knew. Not yet.

At Singh Haveli, Vardaan's days no longer belonged to him. Meetings began before sunrise. Mining disputes. Transport permits. Contract negotiations. Labor strikes. Political demands. Security briefings. Problems arrived faster than solutions. The scientist who once spent his nights studying galaxies now spent his mornings calculating diesel costs and protection routes. Yet something unexpected had happened. He was learning. Fast. Very fast. Vikram had ruled through instinct. Vardaan ruled through systems. Numbers. Patterns. Probabilities. He approached the Empire exactly as he once approached astrophysics. Every problem had variables. Every enemy left signatures. Every war had mathematics. And mathematics rarely lied.

One morning, while reviewing transport reports, Raghunath Singh burst into the conference room. His face had turned pale. Something was wrong. Very wrong.

— Malik!

The room immediately fell silent. Vardaan looked up. Raghunath struggled to breathe. Then finally spoke.

— Munna ke maar delan...

They killed Munna. For a moment nobody moved. The name carried weight. Heavy weight. Munna Yadav. Thirty-eight. Transport contractor. Father of three daughters. One of Vikram's most loyal men. A man who had spent nearly fifteen years protecting Singh supply routes. Not a gangster. Not a killer. A businessman. A loyalist. And now— Dead.

The details arrived shortly afterward. The attack had occurred before dawn. Near an isolated transport crossing outside Nirsa. Munna's convoy had been stopped. His drivers were beaten. His trucks were seized. Then, in front of dozens of witnesses, he was executed. Not robbed. Not kidnapped. Executed. The message had been left painted on a truck container. Large red letters. Visible from hundreds of meters away. "*PRATAP RAJ.*" Silence filled the conference room. The insult wasn't the murder. The insult was the message. This wasn't business. This wasn't a strategy. This was a declaration.

Three hours later, Vardaan arrived at the scene. Aarohi accompanied him. Against his wishes. Against common sense. Against everyone's advice. The road remained blocked. Workers gathered everywhere. Drivers. Villagers. Families. Police. Journalists. Everyone. The atmosphere felt like a funeral. And a warning. At the center stood Munna's eldest daughter. Perhaps fifteen years old. Standing beside her father's covered body. Refusing to cry. Refusing to collapse. Refusing to leave. The sight struck Vardaan harder than expected. Because suddenly he saw himself. Years ago. Standing beside Vikram. Standing beside loss.

Standing beside helplessness. The girl looked directly at him. Not with respect. Not with fear. With expectation. The expectation that rulers fix things. The expectation that kings protect their people. The expectation that had once belonged to Vikram. Now it belonged to him. And for the first time, Vardaan felt the full weight of the throne.

That evening the funeral took place. Thousands attended. Coal workers. Drivers. Laborers. Contractors. Entire villages. The turnout shocked even veteran organizers. As the pyre burned, whispers moved through the crowd. People were watching. Not the funeral. Vardaan. Waiting to see what he would do. Because empires survive on belief. And belief survives in action.

The answer arrived after sunset. Inside the Haveli. An emergency intelligence briefing. Three field informants. Two intercepted phone calls. One captured courier. Together they provided the same information. Munna's killers had gathered inside an abandoned railway loading yard near Chirkunda. Twenty-two armed men. Led by a local enforcer named Jagga Paswan. One of Pratap's most violent lieutenants. The room erupted immediately. Security chiefs demanded retaliation. Contractors demanded revenge. Political allies demanded action. Everyone wanted blood. Vardaan listened quietly. Then asked only one question.

— Police?

The answer came instantly.

— U to bahut pahile khridl gail ba.

Of course. No surprise there. The room waited. The decision belonged to the King.

Near midnight, forty vehicles left Singh territory. No announcements. No publicity. No speeches. Only purpose. For the first time, Vardaan led the operation personally. Not from a control room. Not from a conference table. From the front. The men noticed. And word spread quickly. Malik khud jaa rahe hain. The King himself is coming.

The railway yard sat on the edge of a dried riverbed. Perfect terrain for smugglers. Perfect terrain for ambushes. Perfect terrain for death. The Singh convoy stopped nearly two kilometers away. The security chief approached.

— Order?

Vardaan studied the area through night-vision optics. Counting positions. Watching patrol patterns. Calculating. Thinking. The scientist remained alive inside him. Then he pointed toward three structures. *"Warehouse." "Watchtower." "Fuel depot."* The security chief nodded. Primary targets. But Vardaan wasn't finished.

— Dus Minit bass.

The man frowned.

— Malik?

— das mint ke smy din ki oo log ko surrendar karne ko."

Silence. Nobody expected that. Not from a Singh. Not during a war. Yet the order stood.

A loudspeaker announcement echoed across the yard. Jagga Paswan. Lay down your weapons. Walk out. And you will live. The response came immediately. Laughter. Gunfire. Insults. Exactly as expected. The ten minutes expired. Vardaan checked his watch. Then quietly spoke.

— Start.

What followed lasted less than twelve minutes. Later, dozens would tell different versions. Most exaggerated. Many were invented. The truth was simpler. The Singh Empire struck with overwhelming force. The watchtower fell first. The warehouse second. The fuel depot third. Within minutes resistance collapsed. The yard belonged to Singh forces. The war had produced another lesson. One that every gang in the coal belt would soon learn. Vardaan Singh was not impulsive. Which made him even more dangerous. More than his father Vairav, more than Vikram.

Jagga Paswan was captured alive. Dragged before Vardaan. His face was bruised. His arrogance was broken. Yet even now he laughed. Because he believed something. Something important.

— Pratap bhai tohra ke khatam kari.

Pratap will destroy you. Vardaan said nothing. Jagga continued.

— Tohar bhai mar gail.

Your brother is dead.

— Empire khatam ho gayil."

The Empire is finished. Several Singh men stepped forward angrily. Vardaan stopped them. Then crouched before Jagga. For several moments neither spoke. Then Vardaan quietly asked:

— Pratap kaha ba?

Where is Pratap? Jagga smiled. A dangerous smile. The smile of a man who knows something.

— Tohra soch se bahut nazdeek.

Closer than you think. The answer lingered. Strange. Cryptic. Almost intentional. Before Vardaan could ask more, Jagga laughed again.

— Pratap tu janta na baa.

You don't know Pratap yet.

The sentence froze everyone. Even Aarohi. Even the guards. Even Vardaan. Jagga's smile widened. Then he whispered:

— Galat aadmi ke dhoondhat baa.

You're hunting the wrong man. For a second, the world seemed to stop. Then Jagga suddenly lunged toward a nearby guard. Chaos erupted. A struggle. A weapon discharged. And moments later—Jagga Paswan lay dead. The answer died with him.

On the return journey, nobody spoke much. The victory should have felt satisfying. Instead it felt incomplete. Because Jagga's final words refused to disappear. You're hunting the wrong man. The same implication. Again. Another clue. Another ghost. Another thread leading backward. Toward Pratap. Toward Vairav. Toward Jay Singh Bajwa. Toward a truth everyone seemed desperate to bury.

The next morning newspapers exploded with headlines.

SINGH EMPIRE STRIKES BACK.

COAL WAR ESCALATES.

VARDAAN SINGH LEADS NIGHT OPERATION.

For the first time since Vikram's death, the region felt something it had not felt in months. Certainty. The throne was occupied. The King had arrived.

Yet far away, inside an abandoned church hidden near the Jharkhand border, Pratap Chauhan read those same headlines. One of his men waited nervously nearby.

— Order, Bhai?

Pratap remained silent. Studying the photograph accompanying the article. Vardaan. Standing among workers. Standing among contractors. Standing where Vikram once stood. The resemblance felt almost cruel. For several moments he said nothing. Then finally smiled. Not with anger. Not with hatred. But with sadness. Deep sadness.

— Ab samay aa gayil baa.

The time has come. The lieutenant frowned.

— Kis ka?"

Pratap looked toward the rising sun. Toward the coal belt. Toward the war. Toward history. And quietly answered:

— Use sach batawe ke.

To tell him the truth. Outside, the first colors of this year's Holi advertisements had begun appearing across villages and towns. Nobody noticed them. Nobody paid attention. But destiny had. And somewhere beyond the smoke, beyond the coal, beyond the blood — The road to the Unholy Holi had already begun.

CHAPTER ELEVEN

THE KING & HIS KINGDOM

Bharat Brick Works, May, 2019

The rumors spread faster than bullets. Within forty-eight hours of the Chirkunda operation, every district from Dhanbad to Giridih had heard the same story. Some said Vardaan Singh had led fifty men. Others claimed five hundred. Some said he personally fought Jagga Paswan. Others swore he executed him. The details changed. The legend grew. Only one fact remained constant. *The Singh Empire had struck back.* And for the first time since Vikram's death, fear began changing direction.

At Bharat Brick Works, work continued day and night. Coal trucks moved constantly. Kilns burned without pause. Laborers loaded bricks under clouds of red dust. The Empire was alive. Wounded. But alive. From the upper balcony of the administrative building, Vardaan watched the activity below. Months ago, his mornings began with satellite telemetry and aerospace simulations. Now they began with production reports and security updates. The transformation still felt unreal. Sometimes, late at night, he wondered whether the scientist from America still existed. Or whether that man had already died with Vikram. A voice interrupted his thoughts.

— Malik.

Ramdeen approached. The old caretaker carried a leather file. His expression remained serious. Which usually meant trouble.

— Ka ba?

What is it? Ramdeen handed him the file.

— Teen district ke log milna chahat ba."

People from three districts want to meet you. Vardaan opened the file. Names. Photographs. Background reports. Mine operators. Transport union heads. Regional strongmen. Independent contractors. None of them belonged to Singh territory. Not anymore. For years they had remained neutral. Now they wanted an audience. Interesting. Very interesting.

By noon, the old furnace hall had transformed into a council chamber. The location itself was symbolic. *Bharat Furnace.* The birthplace of the Empire. The place where Vairav Singh and Jay Singh Bajwa had once laid the first bricks. Now another generation gathered there. One by one, the visitors arrived. First came Suryakant Yadav. Owner of three coal loading facilities. Then Mahesh Tiwari. Transport syndicate leader. Then Rajendra Paswan. Former ally of Pratap. Then more. And more. Until nearly twenty influential men filled the hall. Each represented thousands of workers. Millions of rupees. Entire local economies. The atmosphere felt less like a business meeting. And more like a coronation.

Nobody spoke initially. Everyone observed. Measured. Judged. A common ritual in criminal empires. Power had to be evaluated personally. Especially after a succession crisis. Finally, Suryakant stood. The oldest among them. A man who had known Vairav Singh. Known Vikram. Seen empires rise and fall. His eyes remained fixed on Vardaan.

— Hum sidha baat kari?

May I speak directly? Vardaan nodded.

— Hamesha.

The old man smiled slightly.

— Sahi ba.

Then he asked the question everyone had come to ask.

— Tohar raj kitna din tikii?

How long will your rule survive?

The hall became silent. Even the furnace seemed to stop breathing. A challenge. Not disrespectful. Necessary. A test.

Vardaan leaned back. Considering. The scientist in him searched for the correct answer. The king in him understood something deeper. These men didn't need promises. They needed conviction. Finally he spoke.

— Jab tak log saath baa.

As long as the people stand with me. Several men exchanged glances. Unexpected answer. No arrogance. No threats. No grand declarations. Just reality. Then Vardaan continued.

— Empire koi ekan aadmi se na chalta.

An empire doesn't run because of one man.

— Logan se chalta.

It runs because of its people. Now even Suryakant seemed impressed. The room shifted. Slightly. Subtly. But noticeably. The first wall had cracked.

By evening, agreements were signed. Security partnerships. Transport cooperation. Coal distribution contracts. Shared intelligence networks. Nothing official. Nothing legal. Everything is important. One by one, the visitors pledged support. Not because they loved Vardaan. Not because they feared him. Because they believed he could win. And in places like these, belief was currency.

That same evening, Aarohi made a discovery. One that would trouble her deeply. She had spent days examining archived land records connected to Bharat Brick Works. Most documents appeared routine. Ownership transfers. Expansion permits. Industrial registrations. Then she noticed a name. Repeated multiple times. Across multiple decades. Pratap Chauhan. Her eyes narrowed. That shouldn't be possible. Officially, Pratap was never an owner. Never a partner. Never family. Yet his name appeared beside Vairav Singh. Beside Jay Singh Bajwa. Beside the earliest business registrations. Not once. Repeatedly. Almost as though he had always been there. Almost as though history itself had been rewritten later. The realization chilled her. Because it suggested something terrifying. Pratap wasn't an outsider. Pratap might have been one of the founders.

Meanwhile, sixty kilometers away, inside a private estate hidden among sal forests, Jay Singh Bajwa sat alone. The room around him resembled a museum. Photographs. Awards. Political memorabilia. Fragments of a life spent accumulating power. A television played silently in the background. News channels discussed Vardaan's growing influence. The headlines irritated him. Not because they were wrong. Because they were true. The old man poured himself tea. Then studied a photograph hanging on the wall. Vairav Singh. Younger. Smiling. Alive. For a moment something almost human crossed his face. Regret. Then it vanished. A knock interrupted his thoughts. One of his political advisers entered.

— Sir.

Jay Singh Bajwa looked up.

— Bol.

Speak. The adviser hesitated. Then carefully replied:

— chetriy smuh apan smrthn Vardaan ke or ja rahal."

The old man nodded. Expected. Nothing surprising.

— Jaane de.

The adviser frowned. That wasn't the response he anticipated. Jay Singh Bajwa smiled faintly.

— Jitna upar jaayega...

The higher he rises...

The old man paused. Then completed the sentence.

—...utna zor se girega.

...the harder he will fall.

Far away, in an abandoned church near the Jharkhand border, Pratap Chauhan listened to the same news reports. Unlike Bajwa, he smiled. Genuinely smiled. The report described Vardaan as: The New King of the Coal Belt. The title lingered. Because years ago another man had received a similar title. Vikram Singh. Pratap closed his eyes. Memories surfaced. Old memories. Painful memories. Brotherhood. Loyalty. Betrayal. Blood. The past never stayed buried. No matter how hard people tried. One of his lieutenants approached.

— Naya order?

New orders? Pratap looked toward the darkness beyond the church windows.Then slowly shook his head.

— Na.

The lieutenant appeared confused.

— Hum logan hamla na kari?

Pratap smiled faintly.

—Abhi na.

Not yet.

— Kahe?

Pratap's expression hardened. Because the answer carried years of pain.

— Kahe ki Raja ke pehle taaj milna chahi.

A king must first receive his crown. The lieutenant understood nothing. But Pratap wasn't speaking to him. He was speaking to ghosts.

Three days later, Vardaan received an invitation. No signature. No sender. No explanation. Only a location. An abandoned colonial-era bungalow hidden deep inside forest territory near Parasnath Hills. And a time. Midnight. Aarohi immediately objected.

— This is obviously a trap.

Ramdeen agreed. The security chiefs agreed. Everyone agreed. Which was exactly why Vardaan became interested. Because whoever sent it knew something. Or wanted him to know something. The question was what.

Midnight arrived under heavy clouds. The forest seemed endless. Silent. Ancient. Watching. Vardaan arrived with a small security team. No more. Too many men would scare away whoever organized the meeting. The bungalow appeared exactly where the map indicated. Broken walls. Collapsed roof. Decades abandoned. The perfect place for secrets. Inside, a single lantern burned. Nothing else. No people. No voices. No movement. Only a wooden table. And a box. Waiting. Like the photograph. Like the cassette tape. Like every clue before it. Vardaan approached cautiously. Opened the box. And froze. Inside lay an old photograph. Much older than the others. Black and white. Damaged by time. But still recognizable. Vairav Singh. Jay Singh Bajwa. A young Pratap. And standing beside them— A woman. Unknown. Beautiful. Smiling. The photograph alone was surprising. The note attached to it was devastating. Written in red ink. The same handwriting from before. The same invisible messenger. Two words. *Find Savitri*. Nothing more. Nothing less. The lantern flickered. The forest wind howled through broken walls. And somewhere, buried beneath decades of lies, another door had begun to open. A door leading not toward Pratap. Not toward Vikram. But toward the origin. Toward the first betrayal. Who is this Savitri ?

CHAPTER TWELVE

THE GHOSTS OF THE PAST

Bharat Brick Works, , May, 2019

The photograph changed everything. For three days it remained on Vardaan's desk. Three days. Three sleepless nights. Three days of staring at faces that should not have existed together. Vairav Singh. Jay Singh Bajwa. Pratap Chauhan. And the unknown woman. The note attached beneath it contained only two words. *Find Savitri.* Nothing else. No explanation. No sender. No answers. Only another question. Yet Vardaan had learned something important over the previous weeks. The truth never arrived as a whole. It arrived in fragments. Photographs. Cassette tapes. Whispers. Ghosts. And every ghost seemed determined to drag him deeper into the past.

The fourth morning began before sunrise. Rain clouds covered the coal belt. The kilns of Bharat Furnace burned through darkness like giant red eyes. From the balcony outside his office, Vardaan watched workers begin another day. Thousands depended on the Empire. Drivers. Laborers. Contractors. Families. Entire villages. The responsibility felt heavier now. Because the deeper he dug into Vikram's murder, the more he realized something unsettling. The Empire itself might have been built upon a lie. A voice interrupted his thoughts.

— Malik.

Ramdeen. Again. Always appearing whenever the past became uncomfortable. The old caretaker carried a steel tray of tea. His eyes immediately fell upon the photograph resting on the table. For a fraction of a second— Something changed. Fear. Real fear. Then it disappeared. Too late. Vardaan noticed. So did Aarohi.

The office door closed. Silence filled the room. Nobody touched the tea. Nobody sat. Vardaan simply slid the photograph across the desk. Toward Ramdeen.

— Kaun baa ee?

Who is she? The old man's hands trembled. Only slightly. But enough. He stared at the image for a long time. A very long time. Then finally whispered:

— Hum sochni ee sab kabhu laut ke na aayi.

I thought all of this would never return. Aarohi leaned forward immediately.

— aap kya jaante ho Ramdeen?

Ramdeen remained silent. His eyes never left the photograph. Then slowly— Very slowly— He sat down. For the first time since Vikram's death. As though the weight of decades had finally become too much.

Outside, thunder rolled across the coal fields. Inside, another storm began.

— Ee Savitri baa."

This is Savitri. The words landed heavily. Vardaan's pulse quickened. His mother. The woman he barely remembered. The woman whose name nobody spoke anymore. The woman who supposedly died when he was a child. Ramdeen closed his eyes. As though reopening wounds.

— Bahut log kahani jaane la.

Many people know the story.

— Par sach bahut kam log jaane la.

But very few know the truth. The room became completely silent. Even Aarohi stopped taking notes. Instinct told her this mattered. Perhaps more than anything so far.

Ramdeen's voice grew distant. Like a man walking through memory.

— Jab hum jawan rahni...

When I was young...

—...tab Bharat Furnace naya-naya banat rahal.

Bharat Furnace was still being built. Back then, Vairav Singh and Jay Singh Bajwa were inseparable. Not business partners. Not allies. Brothers. The kind of brothers who survived poverty together. Fought together. Bled together. Built together. The entire Empire grew from their friendship. Workers respected both. Villages trusted both. Nobody imagined they could ever stand apart. Then Savitri arrived.

The story unfolded slowly. Painfully. Like old wounds reopening. Savitri wasn't born into power. She came from a schoolteacher's family near Hazaribagh. Educated. Strong-willed. Fearless. Unlike most people, she treated Vairav and Jay Singh Bajwa exactly the same. No fear. No admiration. No special treatment. Perhaps that was why both men admired her. Perhaps that was why everything changed. Ramdeen looked toward the rain outside. Then continued.

— Jay Singh Bajwa bhi unse pyaar karta rahal.

Jay Singh Bajwa loved her too.

The room froze. Vardaan stared. Aarohi stopped breathing. The implication arrived instantly. The beginning. The first fracture. The first crack in the foundation.

— Par Savitri Vairav ke chuni.

But Savitri chose Vairav. Simple words. Devastating consequences. Ramdeen's voice dropped lower.

— Us din kuch toot gayil.

Something broke that day. Not publicly. Not immediately. But inside Jay Singh Bajwa. The old caretaker's eyes grew distant. As though seeing ghosts.

— Hum sab dekhni rahi.

I saw it. The smiles remained. The friendship remained. The Empire continued growing. Yet something had changed. Something dangerous. The kind of change that waits years before revealing itself.

The room remained silent long after Ramdeen finished speaking. Finally Aarohi spoke.

— Phir kya hua?

Ramdeen hesitated. For the first time. Real hesitation. Because what came next frightened him. Even now. Even after decades.

— Hum sab na jaaneeni.

I don't know everything.

—magar...

The word lingered. Dangerously.

— Vairav Singh ke maut ke pahile...

Before Vairav Singh's death...

—...bahut jhagda bhayil.

There were many arguments. Between Vairav. And Jay Singh Bajwa. About money. Territory. Ownership. Power. Nobody knew the details. Only that the friendship had begun dying. Long before Vairav did.

That evening, Vardaan sat alone inside the old furnace chamber. The original furnace. The birthplace of the Empire. The place where everything started. A single lantern illuminated the darkness. The ancient brick walls seemed alive. Watching. Listening. Remembering. For the first time, Vardaan stopped thinking about Pratap. Stopped thinking about revenge. Stopped thinking about territory. Instead he thought about inheritance. Perhaps every generation inherited unfinished wars. Perhaps Vikram inherited Vairav's. Perhaps he inherited Vikram's. Perhaps the dead never truly left. They simply passed their battles forward.

The answer arrived unexpectedly. Near midnight. One of the oldest workers requested an audience. A man named Jagdish. Eighty-two years old. Former furnace operator. One of the original employees. The kind of man history forgets. Yet history often hides inside forgotten men. Jagdish entered slowly. Bent by age. Yet his eyes remained sharp. Very sharp. He looked at the photograph. Then I immediately recognized it.

— nehi kvno dowrahe naikhe.

His voice remained firm.

— Ee Savitri hi baa.

This is Savitri. Then he surprised everyone.

— Humra paas kuch aur bhi baa.

I have something else.

An hour later they arrived at his small house. Located near one of the oldest worker settlements. The place resembled a museum. Old tools. Old photographs. Old documents. Fragments of another era. Jagdish disappeared into a storage room. Returned carrying a rusted metal trunk. Then opened it. Inside rested dozens of photographs. Letters. Newspaper cuttings. Memories. Among them— One item changed everything. A photograph. Another photograph. Taken years after the first one. The image showed: Vairav Singh. Savitri. Young Vikram. Young Vardaan. And standing beside them— Jay Singh Bajwa. Smiling. But someone had scratched his face out. Deliberately. Violently. Repeatedly. The photograph felt less like a family picture. And more like evidence. Evidence of hatred. Evidence of betrayal. Evidence of war.

Then Jagdish revealed something worse. On the back of the photograph— Someone had written a date. And a sentence. In fading blue ink. The date matched exactly three days before Vairav Singh's murder. The sentence contained only five words. *He knows the truth now.* Nobody spoke. Nobody moved. The room seemed to shrink. Because suddenly the timeline changed. If the note was authentic— Then Vairav's death wasn't random. It wasn't business. Wasn't politics. It was connected. Connected to something he discovered. Something dangerous enough to kill for.

As dawn approached, Vardaan and Aarohi returned to Bharat Furnace. Neither spoke much. Both processed the implications. Every revelation pointed backward. Toward Vairav. Toward Savitri. Toward Jay Singh Bajwa. Toward a secret buried beneath decades of blood. Yet one question remained. Who was sending the clues? The photographs. The tapes. The notes. The messages. Someone wanted the truth exposed. But why? And why now?

Far away, inside an abandoned church near the border, Pratap Chauhan stood before a candle-lit altar. The silence around him felt ancient. Almost sacred. One of his lieutenants approached carefully.

— Information pahunch gayil.

The information reached him. Pratap nodded. Expected. Necessary. The lieutenant frowned.

— Ab?

What now? Pratap stared into the darkness. Then quietly answered:

— Ab woh pichhe mud ke dekhega.

Now he will look backward. The lieutenant understood nothing. But Pratap wasn't speaking to him. He was speaking to destiny. Because every road now led toward the same place. Toward Vairav. Toward Savitri. Toward Jay Singh Bajwa. Toward the truth. And truth, once awakened, never sleeps again.

Morning arrived over Bharat Furnace. The kilns burned. The trucks moved. The Empire worked. As if nothing had changed. Yet everything had. Because for the first time since Vikram's death— Vardaan finally understood something. Pratap Chauhan might have killed his brother. But Pratap Chauhan did not create this tragedy. Someone else did. Someone older. Someone smarter. Someone who had been standing beside the family since the very beginning. Someone named— *Jay Singh Bajwa.* And somewhere beyond the smoke of the coal belt, beyond the furnaces, beyond the blood-stained roads— The next war was already waiting. Not a war for territory. Not a war for power. A war for the past.

CHAPTER THIRTEEN

FIRE AND COAL

Dhanbad Coal Belt, June, 2019

The coal belt had its own heartbeat. It did not beat through cities. It beat through mines. Through furnaces. Through railway sidings. Through overloaded trucks that moved like giant black insects across dusty highways. Money flowed through coal. Power flowed through coal. Blood flowed through coal. And in eastern India, whoever controlled coal controlled everything. For months after Vikram Singh's death, that heartbeat had become irregular. Fear had entered the system. Contractors stopped paying. Transport operators changed loyalties. Mine owners began negotiating with multiple factions. The Empire still existed. But people no longer believed it was immortal. And belief was the first thing a king must recover.

Bharat Furnace

The morning council meeting had barely begun when chaos entered the room. Three contractors arrived together. Covered in coal dust. Exhausted. Terrified. One of them, Mahendra Gupta, nearly collapsed before reaching the conference table. Vardaan immediately stood.

— ka bhyil?

The man struggled to catch his breath.

Then finally spoke.

— Malik...

His voice shook.

— Kal raat hamaar mine par hamla bhayil.

Last night my mine was attacked. The room fell silent. Another contractor stepped forward.

— Humar bhi.

Mine too. Then the third.

— Hamaar loading yard jala dehal.

My loading yard was burned down. Ramdeen exchanged a glance with the security chiefs. Nobody needed further explanation. Everyone already knew whose signature this was. Pratap Chauhan. Maps were spread across the conference table. Attack locations marked in red. Three mines. Two stockyards. One transport checkpoint. The pattern emerged immediately. These weren't random attacks. These were strategic strikes. Every target had one thing in common. They had recently requested protection from the Singh Empire. Pratap wasn't stealing territory. He was discouraging loyalty. Sending a message. Anyone who stands with Vardaan Singh will suffer. The room erupted into arguments.

— hamni ke turnt jvabee karyvai ke jrurat ba.

— inka depo jala de

— unkar fainensar ke mar din.

Voices rose. Tempers flared. The atmosphere grew increasingly volatile. Vardaan remained silent. Studying the map. Studying the numbers. Studying the pattern. The scientist inside him noticed something. The targets formed a corridor. Not random. Purposeful. A coal corridor. A route connecting four major mines to railway loading points. The realization arrived instantly. Pratap wasn't attacking contractors. He was preparing to seize supply lines. The war had entered a new phase.

Vardaan slowly stood. The room quieted immediately. A few months ago nobody would have waited for his decision. Now everyone does. The realization gave him an unexpected sensation. Power. Pure power. Not physical. Not political. Psychological. Dozens of influential men waiting for a single sentence. A single decision. A single command. For a moment he understood why men like Vairav Singh and Jay Singh Bajwa spent entire lifetimes chasing authority. Because authority was intoxicating. More addictive than alcohol. More seductive than love. More dangerous than violence. Vardaan pushed the thought away. Then spoke.

—ham intzar nai karenge.

The room leaned forward.

— hamla aju rat hi hoghi

By afternoon, a convoy of nearly fifty vehicles moved into the mining belt. News travelled faster than the convoy itself. Workers lined roads. Truck drivers stopped to watch. Tea stalls buzzed with rumors. Vardaan Singh was coming personally. Not sending representatives. Not sending gunmen. Coming himself again. The effect was immediate. Morale surged. Because in regions abandoned by government and law, presence mattered more than promises.

The first mine stood near the edge of a massive open-cast excavation. Thousands worked there. Coal dust covered everything. The air itself seemed black. As Vardaan stepped out of his vehicle, workers began gathering. Hundreds at first. Then thousands. Many had never met him. Yet they stared at him as though looking at Vikram reborn. Some saw Vairav. Some saw hope. Others simply saw survival. The mine manager approached nervously.

— Malik, situation kharab baa.

The situation is bad.

— adha mazdoor chhodal chaht ba."

Vardaan looked around. Fear was visible everywhere. People didn't believe the Empire could protect them. That was the real problem. Not Pratap. Fear. And fear spread faster than bullets.

Vardaan climbed onto an old loading platform. The workers fell silent. Thousands of faces looked upward. Waiting. Expecting. Judging. For several moments he said nothing. Then spoke. Without microphones. Without prepared speeches. Without political language. Simple words.

— Batawa.

Tell me.

— Ee mine ke malik kaun baa?

Who owns this mine?

The crowd exchanged confused glances. One worker shouted.

— Company!

Laughter followed. Vardaan smiled. Then shook his head.

— Nahi.

"No."

He pointed toward the workers.

— Tohra log.

You people. The crowd became silent again. Vardaan continued.

— Company paisa lagawe la.

The company invests money.

— Hum security dewe tani.

I provide security.

— Par kaam ke karela?

But who does the work? The workers answered together.

— Hum!

Us!

Vardaan nodded.

— Haan!

Then his voice hardened.

— Jab tak hum zinda hai...

As long as I am alive...

—..ee mine par kehu kabja na kari.

No one will take this mine. Thunderous applause erupted. The effect was immediate. Not because of the words. Because he had come. Personally.

That evening, another surprise awaited him. The largest labor gathering in the region assembled outside the mine. Thousands upon thousands of workers. Miners. Drivers. Loaders. Mechanics. Families. Entire communities. What began as a spontaneous gathering quickly transformed into something larger. Something symbolic. Something dangerous. An old union leader stepped forward. His face carried decades of coal dust and hardship. He looked directly at Vardaan. Then raised a black coal-covered fist.

— Vikram ke baad...

After Vikram...The crowd fell silent. The old man continued.

— Koyla ke raja ke kursi khaali rahal.

The throne of the coal belt remained empty. Then he pointed toward Vardaan.

— Aaj se na.

Not anymore. The crowd exploded. Thousands of voices. One chant. Growing louder. And louder. And louder.

— Koyla ke raja!

— Koyla ke raja!

— Koyla ke raja!

The words echoed across the mine. Across the valley. Across the blackened earth. Vardaan stood motionless. But inside— Something changed. Something dangerous. Because for the first time, he liked it. The title. The loyalty. The worship. He liked it. Far more than he should have.

Later that night, back at Singh Haveli, Aarohi continued her investigation. Boxes of old records surrounded her. Photographs. Employee registers. Land deeds. Transport contracts. Fragments of forgotten history. Most appeared useless. Then she found another photograph. And froze. The image was old. Very old. Perhaps twenty-five years. Maybe more. A group photograph taken near Bharat Furnace. Workers standing together. Managers standing together. Young Vairav Singh. Young Jay Singh Bajwa. And among them— A teenage boy. Thin. Sharp-eyed. Standing beside Vairav. The same face. Older now. Hardened now. But unmistakable. *Pratap*. A young Pratap Chauhan. A teenager. Inside Bharat Furnace. Decades before anyone claimed he entered the family's life. Aarohi stared at the image. Her pulse accelerated. This wasn't a coincidence. This wasn't a casual connection. Pratap hadn't infiltrated the Empire. He belonged to it. The realization felt explosive. Because it shattered the official story. Every version of history suddenly looked suspicious.

Far away, inside an abandoned church near the border, Pratap Chauhan sat alone. A lantern flickered nearby. Rain tapped softly against stained glass. One of his lieutenants entered.

— News aa gayil.

The news has arrived. Pratap looked up.

— Ka news?

The lieutenant smiled nervously.

— Log unke Koyla Ka Raja bulawe lagal ba.

People have started calling him the Coal Belt King. For a long moment, Pratap said nothing. Then something unexpected happened. He laughed. A genuine laugh. Warm. Almost affectionate. The lieutenant looked confused. Pratap slowly leaned back. His eyes drifted toward the darkness. Toward memory. Toward another time. Another king. Another brother. Then he whispered softly. Almost to himself.

— Bilkul Vikram jaisan...

Just like Vikram...

The smile slowly disappeared. Replaced by sadness. Deep sadness. Because Pratap knew something Vardaan didn't. Every Singh who sat on that throne eventually paid for it. And history was already preparing the bill.

As dawn approached, coal trains departed once again from the mining belt. The supply corridor survived. The workers celebrated. The contractors felt protected. The Empire expanded. The throne strengthened. The legend grew. But beneath the coal. Beneath the power. Beneath the applause. Old ghosts continued to move. Savitri. Vairav. Pratap. Jay Singh Bajwa. And somewhere inside the darkness of the past, a truth waited patiently. Watching. Until the day it would finally destroy them all.

CHAPTER FOURTEEN

The Highway Kingdom

Grand Trunk Road, July, 2019

The old Grand Trunk Road had existed long before empires. Before governments. Before borders. Before the Singh Empire. For centuries it connected kingdoms, merchants, armies, pilgrims, smugglers and conquerors. Now it carried something equally valuable. Coal. And wherever coal traveled, money followed. Where money followed, power followed. And where power followed—Blood was never far behind.

Bharat Furnace

The emergency council meeting began before sunrise. Unlike previous meetings, the atmosphere felt different. More dangerous. Coal mines could survive temporary disruptions. Transport networks could not. If trucks stopped moving, the Empire stopped breathing. Maps covered the entire conference table. Highways. State roads. Loading stations. Railway crossings. Fuel depots. Checkpoints. Every artery feeding the Singh Empire. And every artery was under attack. Ramdeen pointed toward multiple red circles.

— Kal raat chhe truck jala dehal gail.

Six trucks were burned last night. Another officer spoke.

— Dhanbad route par extortion shuru ho gayil baa.

Extortion has started on the Dhanbad route. Another voice joined.

— Driver log kaam chhorat baa.

Drivers are quitting. The room erupted. Everybody spoke at once. Nobody had solutions. Because transportation was different from mining. A mine could be guarded. A highway stretched for hundreds of kilometers. You couldn't protect every mile. At least not traditionally.

Vardaan listened quietly. The scientist inside him was still alive. Still calculating. Still observing patterns. He studied the attack locations. The timing. The routes. The affected operators. Then he noticed something. Pratap wasn't trying to destroy transport. He was fragmenting it. Dividing it. Making syndicates distrust each other. Making drivers fear every route. Making contractors negotiate separately. Classic divide-and-rule. The realization came instantly. The Empire didn't need more guns. It needed unity.

Vardaan slowly stood. The room fell silent. That silence still fascinated him. Months ago nobody cared about his opinion. Now fifty powerful men stopped speaking whenever he stood. The feeling had become familiar. Dangerously familiar.

— hamni ye sistm bdl rahal.

The room waited.

— ab koi swtntr transport contract na hoi."

Several contractors immediately protested.

— Ka?

— Namumkin.

— bahute mahanga ba

— Logistics collapse ho jaayi.

The system will collapse.

Vardaan shook his head.

— Na.

Then pointed toward the map.

— Ab se sab route ek network ke andar aayi.

From now on every route enters one network. No separate security. No separate convoys. No separate negotiations. One system. One protection. One command. One Empire. The room slowly understood. He wasn't responding to the crisis. He was restructuring the kingdom.

By afternoon, news spread through the coal belt. The Singh Empire had launched a Unified Logistics Network. For the first time in decades: Mine operators. Truck owners. Warehouse managers. Loading contractors. Fuel suppliers. All came under one protection framework. Economically, it was brilliant. Politically, it was revolutionary. Criminally, it was terrifying. Because now every attack against a single truck became an attack against everyone.

Not everyone welcomed the idea. Especially not those already working with Pratap. That evening, inside a roadside dhaba near Topchanchi, a meeting took place. Transport syndicate leaders sat around a long table. Arguments filled the room. Some wanted Singh protection. Others wanted neutrality. Others secretly worked for Pratap. The division became obvious. And division was exactly what Pratap wanted. A middle-aged transport operator slammed his fist against the table.

— Hum Singh ke saath jaat bani.

I'm joining the Singhs. Immediately another man stood.

— Pagal ho gayil baa?

Have you gone mad?

— Pratap se takkar leba?

You'll challenge Pratap? The argument escalated. Threats followed. Then chairs overturned. Within seconds the meeting dissolved into violence. The transport world had officially split. The war had begun.

Three nights later, the first major confrontation arrived. A convoy carrying high-grade coal left Dhanbad after sunset. Thirty-seven trucks. Destination: Industrial processing facilities near Asansol. Estimated cargo value: Several crores. The convoy represented more than coal. It represented confidence. If it reached safely, Vardaan's new network survived. If it failed, the entire initiative collapsed. Which was why Pratap chose that convoy.

The attack began near midnight. A lonely stretch of GT Road. Dense forest on both sides. Minimal police presence. Perfect terrain. The lead truck suddenly exploded into flames. Not a bomb. A fuel tanker rammed directly into it. The road became an inferno. Brakes screamed. Drivers panicked. Trucks stopped. Chaos erupted. Then gunfire began. From both sides of the highway.

The ambush was professional. Fast. Coordinated. Merciless. Masked gunmen emerged from darkness. Vehicles were hijacked. Drivers dragged out. Convoy security struggled to respond. Everything happened within minutes. Exactly according to Pratap's plan. What the attackers didn't anticipate was one thing. Vardaan himself.

Two hours earlier, intelligence had reached Bharat Furnace. A possible attack. Most leaders would've stayed behind. Issued orders remotely. Not Vardaan. Not anymore. By the time the ambush began, he was already en route. Because increasingly, Vardaan preferred direct intervention. The danger excited him. The control excited him. The feeling of deciding life and death excited him. Though he would never admit it. Not yet.

His convoy arrived just as the firefight intensified. The scene resembled a battlefield. Burning trucks. Smoke. Screaming men. Automatic gunfire. The night itself seemed on fire. Without hesitation Vardaan stepped out. Ignoring protests. Ignoring security warnings. Ignoring common sense.

— Position lo!

Take positions! His men spread rapidly. Returning fire. The battle expanded across both sides of the highway. Bullets shattered windshields. Engines exploded. Coal spilled across the road. For nearly forty minutes the fight continued. Brutal. Confusing. Relentless. Eventually the attackers broke. Retreated into the forest. Disappearing as quickly as they had arrived. Leaving behind bodies. Burned vehicles. And a message. The transport war was now official.

By dawn, news channels had arrived. Drone footage captured the destruction. Burned trucks lined the highway. Workers gathered in thousands. Reporters interviewed drivers. Every answer sounded similar.

— Vardaan Singh khud aaye rahin.

Vardaan Singh came himself.

— Humra jaan bachwaile.

He saved our lives.

— He stood with us.

The narrative spread instantly. Not a businessman. Not a gangster. Not an employer. Protector. The distinction mattered. Because legends are built on perception. Not facts.

Later that day, Vardaan visited a temporary workers' camp. Many injured drivers had gathered there. Some received treatment. Others simply rested. As he walked through the camp, something unexpected happened. People stood. One after another. Then more. Then everyone. Nobody instructed them. Nobody organized it. They simply stood. Out of respect. Out of gratitude. Out of belief. The effect was overwhelming. Thousands of tired workers standing for one man. Vardaan felt it again. That dangerous feeling. The feeling is growing stronger with every passing week. The feeling that perhaps— Just perhaps— The Empire needed him. Not wanted. Needed. And once a man starts believing he is indispensable, he becomes capable of almost anything.

That evening, Aarohi continued examining old archives. The photograph from Bharat Furnace refused to leave her mind. Teenage Pratap. Standing beside Vairav. Years before official history. The inconsistency bothered her. Deeply. So she kept digging. Hours later she discovered another photograph. Then another. Then another. The pattern became undeniable. Pratap appeared repeatedly throughout the records. Factory celebrations. Worker gatherings. Annual functions. Land ceremonies. Always somewhere nearby. Never identified. Never mentioned. Yet always present. Almost like family. A cold realization spread through her. Someone had deliberately erased him from history. The question wasn't why Pratap became an enemy. The question was: "*Why had the family pretended he was never part of them?*"

Far away, inside the abandoned church near the border, Pratap Chauhan listened to reports from the convoy battle. His lieutenant appeared frustrated.

— We lost men.

Pratap nodded.

Expected.

— We lost vehicles.

Again, expected. The lieutenant finally asked:

— Kahe rok na detani unke?

Why don't you stop him? Pratap remained silent. For a long moment. Then looked toward an old photograph resting beside a candle. A photograph nobody else was allowed to touch. The image had faded badly. But one face remained visible. Vikram Singh. Young. Laughing. Alive. Pratap stared at it. Then quietly answered.

— Abhi na.

Not yet. The lieutenant frowned.

— Why?

Pratap's eyes never left the photograph. Because some wars weren't fought to win. Some wars were fought to reveal the truth. And the truth was finally beginning to move.

Back at Bharat Furnace, night settled over the coal kingdom. Trains continued moving. Convoys resumed operation. The highways survived. The network survived. The Empire grew stronger. And standing on the rooftop of Bharat Furnace, looking across the endless industrial landscape, Vardaan Singh allowed himself a dangerous thought. Perhaps Vikram had protected the kingdom. Perhaps Vairav had built the kingdom. But he— He was destined to rule it. The idea stayed with him long after midnight. Like coal beneath ash. Waiting. Growing hotter. Preparing for the fire to come.

CHAPTER FIFTEEN

The Minister's Son

Patna – Dhanbad – GT Road Corridor, July, 2019,

Power in the coal belt did not wear one face. Sometimes it wore a miner's helmet. Sometimes it wore a gangster's scar. Sometimes it wore a politician's smile. Vardaan understood this clearly now. The transport war had stabilized after the GT Road battle, but another problem emerged immediately. Trucks were being stopped at state checkpoints. Permits were being delayed. Coal consignments were being seized for "inspection." Not by Pratap's men. By the government. Or rather, by the men who owned the government. At Bharat Furnace, the morning briefing carried a different kind of tension. No gunfire reports. No ambushes. Only files. And files, Vardaan was learning, could cripple an empire more effectively than bullets. A senior transport officer spread documents across the table.

— Maalik, du din men byalis trak hirasat men le li.

Another added,

— raton rat nya aadesh jari karel"

A third man lowered his voice.

— Patna se pressure aa raha hai.

Pressure from Patna. The room fell silent. Everyone knew what that meant. Politics had entered the war.

Ramdeen spoke quietly.

— Minister Raghubir Prasad.

The name carried weight across Bihar and Jharkhand. Coal, transport, contracts, police postings, elections—his reach touched everything. But the real problem was not the minister. It was his son. A spoiled, violent man named Aditya Prasad.

Thirty-two years old. Educated abroad. Returned to India with entitlement instead of wisdom. He treated the coal belt like inherited property. And lately, he had started appearing at transport checkpoints personally. Collecting "fees." Humiliating contractors. Forcing drivers to kneel on highways. A contractor named Suresh Yadav stood from his chair, fury shaking his voice.

— Malik, kal humke sabke saamne thappad mar dehal.

Yesterday he slapped me in front of everyone. The room erupted in anger. Another contractor added:

— Bolata— 'Singh Raj khatam ho gayil. Ab Patna Raj chalega.'"

He said, "Singh rule is over. Now Patna rule will run." Vardaan's eyes hardened. Not because of the insult. Because humiliation was strategic. Aditya was trying to prove that the Empire could no longer protect its own men. The same tactic Pratap used. Different clothes. Same war.

After the meeting, Aarohi entered Vikram's old office carrying another folder of archival photographs.

But before discussing them, she studied Vardaan carefully.

— You're changing.

He looked up from the transport maps.

— People keep saying that.

— Because it's true.

She placed a photograph on the desk. A young Pratap standing beside Vairav Singh at a furnace inauguration ceremony.

— I've confirmed it now

she said quietly.

— Pratap was inside the family system from the beginning.

Vardaan's jaw tightened.

— Then why did everyone erase him from history?

— That's the question.

Aarohi paused, then added softly:

— And another question—why is Jay Singh Bajwa never surprised when these revelations appear?

The room grew still. Vardaan looked away. Because somewhere inside him, the suspicion had already begun growing. The decision came that evening.

Vardaan would go to Patna personally. His advisers opposed it immediately.

— bahute jokhim wala kaam hoga ba yeh.

— Yeh ek Political trap hai Maalik.

— vakil log ekra ke sambhale din Malik.

But Vardaan had learned something from Vikram's world. Distance creates weakness. Presence creates authority. Two days later, a convoy of black SUVs entered Patna. The city buzzed instantly. Coal Belt King arrives in the capital. The phrase spread through political circles before he even reached the minister's bungalow.

Raghubir Prasad received him with practiced warmth. The bungalow smelled of sandalwood, expensive liquor, and corruption polished into respectability.

— Arre Vardaan babu! Aap aaye, ghar roshan ho gaya.

The minister embraced him theatrically. Vardaan smiled politely. The performance had begun. They sat in a private chamber lined with political photographs—prime ministers, chief ministers, election rallies, garlands, power frozen in frames. Tea arrived. Then Aditya entered. No greeting. No respect. Only arrogance. He dropped into a chair and smirked.

— So the scientist finally became a gangster.

The room tightened. Even the minister looked uncomfortable. Vardaan remained calm.

— And you? Still collecting toll tax on highways like a roadside thief?

Aditya laughed loudly.

— This is politics, Mr. Singh. Everything has a price.

Vardaan leaned forward.

— Good. Then let's discuss the price.

For the next hour, the conversation moved like a chess match. The minister wanted money. Political funding. Election support. Influence in transport unions. In return, the government pressure would ease. A familiar Indian arrangement. Business dressed as governance. Vardaan understood the game immediately. But then Aditya made a mistake. He leaned back and said casually:

— Waise bhi, Pratap bhai kaafi samajhdaar aadmi hai. Deal karna jaante hain.

"Pratap bhai" is a very intelligent man. He knows how to make deals. The room went silent. Raghubir Prasad's face changed instantly. Too late. Vardaan noticed. Of course he noticed. The scientist in him never stopped observing micro-reactions. Aditya realized his mistake, but arrogance pushed him forward.

— Aap log sochte hain war sirf bandook se hota hai? Naahi."

You think wars are fought only with guns? No They're not.

Vardaan slowly stood. The meeting was over.

— Minister saab,"

he said calmly,

— main deal karne aaya tha.

I came here to make a deal. Then he looked directly at Aditya.

— Lekin aapke bete ne negotiation ko personal bana diya.

But your son has made this personal.

The message arrived the next night. A Singh convoy had been stopped near a highway checkpoint outside Gaya. Drivers beaten. Coal seized. Contractors were forced to kneel on the road while Aditya's men filmed videos on mobile phones. The clips spread across WhatsApp groups within hours. Humiliation had gone digital. At Bharat Furnace, fury exploded.

— Ab bas!

— Order dijiye, Malik!

— Patna jala denge!

But Vardaan was no longer reacting emotionally. He was becoming colder. More precise. He studied the checkpoint location, police deployment, and convoy timings. Then he issued orders.

Quietly. Methodically.

Night on the Highway

At 1:40 a.m., the checkpoint looked routine. Police barricades. A few government vehicles. Armed guards drinking tea under yellow floodlights. Then the darkness moved. Fifteen black SUVs emerged from the highway fog without headlights. The barricades were surrounded before the police understood what was happening. No shots fired initially. Just speed, coordination, and terror. Vardaan stepped out first. The checkpoint officer trembled visibly.

— S-sir... yeh government operation hai...

Vardaan walked past him. Inside the temporary office sat Aditya Prasad. Drunk. Laughing with local officers. Until the door opened. The laughter died instantly. For several seconds, nobody spoke. Then Aditya stood slowly.

— Tum yahan kya kar rahe ho?

What are you doing here? Vardaan looked around the room. On one table lay confiscated Singh transport papers. On another, cash bundles. Extortion money. He picked up a bundle and dropped it back onto the table.

— Politics ka rate achha chal raha hai. Hai na ?

Politics is paying well isn't it ?

Aditya tried to recover his arrogance.

— Tumhe lagta hai tum mujhe dara doge?"

You think you can scare me? Vardaan stepped closer. Very close. His voice dropped to a whisper.

— Nahi.

No. A pause.

— Main tumhe yaad rehne wala dard dene aaya hoon.

I came to give you the pain that you'll remember. What happened next was fast and brutal. Vardaan didn't kill him. That would create a martyr. Instead, he ordered every seized truck released immediately, every officer disarmed, and every extortion ledger confiscated. Then, in front of the same drivers Aditya had humiliated, Vardaan asked everyone to take videos and slapped him once across the face. Then again. And again, and again. Till his cheeks turn red. Not rage. Judgment. The highway froze. No one moved. No one breathed. Vardaan looked at the drivers.

— Utho.

Stand up. They rose slowly. Then he turned back to Aditya.

— Agli baar Singh ke truck roka, toh checkpoint to kya ye pura zilla nahin bachega.

Next time you stop a Singh truck, the checkpoint as well as the whole district won't survive.

By morning, the story had spread everywhere. Some called it madness. Others called it justice. But across the coal belt, one thing became certain: Vardaan Singh had slapped the son of a cabinet minister on a state highway and walked away untouched.

The myth expanded overnight. At tea stalls, truck stops, and mining camps, workers repeated the story with pride.

— Malik khud gail rahin.

The King himself went.

— Aditya ke saamne jhukwa dehal.

He made Aditya bow. For the first time, Vardaan realized something unsettling. The people no longer saw him as a man. They were beginning to see him as an idea. And ideas are harder to control than empires.

That evening, Aarohi entered his office pale and shaken. She carried a newly restored photograph.

— I found this in an old press archive in Patna, she said.

The image showed a political fundraiser from the early 1990s. Vairav Singh. Jay Singh Bajwa. Several ministers. And standing beside them— a teenage Pratap Chauhan wearing a Singh Foundation badge. Vardaan stared at the photograph for a long time.

Then quietly asked:

— Why would my father put Pratap beside politicians?

Aarohi answered softly:

— Because he wasn't just an employee.

The room fell silent. Outside, coal trucks rumbled through the night like distant thunder. Inside, another truth moved closer. And somewhere beyond the highways, beyond the politics, beyond the growing empire, destiny continued building the road toward the Unholy Holi.

CHAPTER SIXTEEN

THE GHOST FILES

Bharat Furnace, August, 2019.

The dead were speaking. Not through ghosts. Not through dreams. Not through superstition. Through documents. Photographs. Signatures. Land deeds. Old files buried beneath decades of dust. And with every new discovery, Aarohi became increasingly convinced of one terrifying possibility. The official history of the Singh Empire was a lie.

The archive room occupied the oldest section of Bharat Furnace. Originally built during the early expansion years of the Empire, it had become little more than a forgotten warehouse. Steel shelves lined the walls. Thousands of files rested beneath decades of dust. Most employees avoided the room. History had little value in a kingdom obsessed with survival. Aarohi disagreed. History explained everything. Especially crimes. Especially betrayals. Especially families. And the Singh family possessed all three.

For three weeks she barely left the archives. Workers brought food. Assistants delivered documents. Researchers restored photographs. Every day she dug deeper. Every day the story became stranger. The pattern was undeniable now. Pratap Chauhan appeared everywhere. Old photographs. Land registrations. Construction permits. Transport contracts. Foundation ceremonies. School inaugurations. Hospital donations. He appeared repeatedly throughout the Empire's history. Yet officially— He didn't exist. At least not according to the records everyone acknowledged. Someone had erased him. Not completely. But carefully. Strategically. Enough to rewrite memory. Not enough to erase the truth.

One afternoon she carried a stack of files directly to Vardaan's office. He sat behind Vikram's old desk. The desk felt natural now. Comfortable. Months ago he still looked like an outsider occupying borrowed space. Now he looked exactly where he belonged. That realization disturbed Aarohi more than she expected. Power was changing him. Quietly. Relentlessly.

She dropped three photographs onto the table.

— Look.

Vardaan studied them. The first showed Vairav Singh at a hospital inauguration. The second showed Bharat Furnace's expansion ceremony. The third captured a political fundraiser from the early nineties. Different years. Different events. Different locations. Yet the same face appeared in every frame. Young Pratap. Always nearby. Always close to the family. Almost like a son. Vardaan stared at the photographs. Then quietly asked:

— How many have you found?

Aarohi answered immediately.

— Thirty-eight.

The room fell silent. Thirty-eight. Not one. Not two. Thirty-eight separate appearances. That wasn't a coincidence. That wasn't an association. That was belonging.

Vardaan leaned back slowly. Something about the photographs bothered him. Not just Pratap. Something else. Then suddenly he noticed. In every image— Pratap stood beside Vikram. Not Vairav. Not Jay Singh Bajwa. Vikram. Always Vikram. The realization arrived like lightning.

— Zoom this.

Aarohi handed him an enlarged print. He examined it carefully. Then another. Then another. The same result. Again. And again. And again. The boys were inseparable. The evidence became impossible to ignore. Pratap wasn't merely connected to the family. He had grown up with Vikram.

— Toh phir...

Vardaan whispered. Then what happened? Neither of them had an answer. Yet.

That evening another discovery arrived. This time from an unlikely source. An eighty-year-old retired accountant named Shyamlal Mishra. One of the last surviving employees from the Empire's earliest years. When he learned Aarohi was researching old records, he requested a meeting. His hands shook with age. His memory did not.

The old man sat quietly inside the archive room. Studying the photographs spread across the table. Eventually he pointed toward one. A faded image taken during a school sports event. Young Vikram. Young Pratap. Both covered in mud. Both laughing. Both holding the same trophy. The old accountant smiled sadly.

— Ee dono alag na rahin.

Those two were never separate. Aarohi immediately leaned forward.

— Aap Unhe jante thein?

The old man nodded.

— Hum sab jaaneeni.

I knew all of them. Then he looked directly at Vardaan. And spoke words that changed everything.

— Pratap ke log naukar bolat baa.

People call Pratap a servant. He shook his head.

— Galat.

Wrong. Then quietly added:

— U ghar ke beta jaisan rahal.

He was like a son of that house.

The room became silent. Even Vardaan stopped moving, how could he never notice that? The old man continued.

— Vikram aur Pratap saath khana khat rahin.

They ate together.

— Saath padhat rahin.

Studied together.

— Saath ladat rahin.

Fought together.

— Saath sapna dekhte rahin.

Dreamed together. The image emerging was completely different from everything Vardaan believed. No infiltrator. No opportunist. No outsider. Pratap had grown up inside the Singh household. Like family.

Then came the most disturbing revelation. The accountant removed a small notebook from his pocket. Ancient. Worn. Nearly falling apart. His personal journal. Inside were handwritten notes dating back decades. One entry caught Aarohi's attention immediately. A date. A sentence. Simple. Yet explosive.

"Master Vikram and Master Pratap left together for Ranchi bidding."

Aarohi reread it twice. Then three times. The implication was obvious. Pratap received the same importance as Vikram. The same opportunities. The same upbringing. Which raised an even bigger question. If he was family— Why was he erased?

Outside, a storm gathered over Bharat Furnace. Coal dust swirled through the air. Thunder rolled across the horizon. The atmosphere felt strangely appropriate. Because another storm was forming inside the Empire. A storm made of memory.

That night Vardaan sat alone inside the old furnace chamber. The original furnace. The birthplace of everything. The same place where Vairav Singh and Jay Singh Bajwa had built their dream. He spread the photographs across the floor. Dozens of them. Fragments of another life. Another version of history. One image kept drawing his attention. Young Vikram. Young Pratap, wearing a jersey with other team mates, probably won the local shield final. Standing shoulder to shoulder. Smiling. Brothers. Not by blood. But something close. Very close. Vardaan stared at the photograph for a long time. Then quietly asked the darkness:

— Why?

Why would a brother kill a brother? The answer arrived unexpectedly. Near midnight. Ramdeen. Again. The keeper of forgotten truths. The old caretaker entered carrying a metal box.

Small. Locked. Ancient. His expression looked troubled. Deeply troubled.

— Ee humra paas bahut saal se baa.

I've had this for many years. He placed the box on the table. Neither Vardaan nor Aarohi spoke. Ramdeen continued.

— Vikram humke dehal rahin.

Vikram gave this to me. The room froze. Immediately. Completely.

Vardaan stood. His pulse accelerated.

— Kab?"

Ramdeen swallowed.

— Marne se kuch mahina pahile.

A few months before he died. The old caretaker looked exhausted. As though carrying the burden had become unbearable.

— He told me...

Ramdeen paused.

—...if something happened to him, this should reach you.

Silence. Absolute silence. Slowly, Vardaan opened the box. Inside rested several items. Old letters. Photographs. A cassette tape. And one sealed envelope. On the front, written in Vikram's handwriting: *FOR VARDAAN*. The room stopped breathing.

His hands trembled slightly. Not from fear. From anticipation. The tape recorder was brought immediately. The cassette inserted. For several seconds only static emerged. Then— A voice. Vikram's voice. Alive. Warm. Familiar. The voice of a dead man.

— Vardaan...

Static. Then again.

— Jab tu ee sunat ho...

If you're hearing this...

— ...tab kuch bahut galat ho chuka hoga.

Something has gone terribly wrong.

Vardaan closed his eyes. The sound hit harder than any bullet ever could. For a moment he wasn't the Coal King. Wasn't the head of an empire. Wasn't a feared ruler. He was simply a younger brother again. Listening to his elder brother. One last time.

The recording continued. Then suddenly— The tape ended. Abruptly. Incomplete. As though someone had stopped it deliberately. Or damaged it. The room sat in stunned silence. The message wasn't finished. The answers remained hidden. Yet one thing became certain. Vikram knew something before he died. Something serious enough to record. Something serious enough to leave behind.

Far away, inside the abandoned church near the border, Pratap Chauhan sat alone. Rain struck stained glass windows. Lightning illuminated the room. One of his men approached.

— Naya khabar baa.

There is new information. Pratap looked up.

— Kya?

The lieutenant answered quietly.

— u log ke vikram ke u dabba milal."

For the first time in months— Pratap's expression changed. Real emotion. Real concern.

He stood immediately. The lieutenant looked surprised. Pratap never reacted this way. Never. Yet now he stared into darkness. As though seeing the future. And perhaps he was. Because he understood something nobody else did. If Vardaan opened the right files... If he found the right names... If he discovered the right truth... Then the war would stop being about territory. And start becoming something far more dangerous. Family.

As thunder shook the coal belt, Vardaan remained seated before the unfinished recording. Listening again. And again. And again. Searching for clues. Searching for meaning. Searching for his brother. Unaware that the answers he sought were no longer hidden inside mines. Or highways. Or transport networks. They were hidden inside the Singh family itself. And every road now pointed toward the same destination. Jay Singh Bajwa.

CHAPTER SEVENTEEN

THE THRONE

Bharat Furnace, September, 2019

There were kingdoms built from gold. Kingdoms built from faith. Kingdoms built from armies. The Singh Empire had been built from something far less noble. Coal. Dust. Blood. Fear. And loyalty. Especially loyalty. For nearly four decades, the Empire had expanded like wildfire across the coal belt. Mines. Brick kilns. Transport routes. Arms networks. Land syndicates. Political channels. Everything connected. Everything is profitable. Everything is dangerous. Yet despite its vast reach, the Empire had one weakness. It was never truly centralized. Vairav Singh ruled through respect. Vikram ruled through trust. Both methods worked. Until betrayal arrived. Vardaan intended to rule differently.

For the first time since Vikram's death, every major stakeholder of the Empire had been summoned. Coal operators. Transport heads. Political intermediaries. Security chiefs. Contractors. Regional enforcers. More than eighty men occupied the chamber. The atmosphere felt historic. Nobody knew why they had been called. Only that Vardaan himself had ordered the meeting. And when Vardaan called— People came.

The room fell silent as he entered. The silence no longer surprised him. Instead, he had begun expecting it. That realization bothered him. Yet it also pleased him. A dangerous combination. He stood at the head of the table. Behind him hung an enormous map of eastern India. Jharkhand. Bihar. West Bengal. Odisha. Every district was touched by the Singh Empire. Every route. Every mine. Every furnace. Every source of power.

— Bahut saal se...

For many years... His voice echoed through the room.

— ...hum log empire chalawat bani.

We have been running an empire. Several heads nodded. Vardaan continued.

— Problem ee ba ki empire chalawat bani...

The problem is that we are running an empire...

—...jaise gaon chalawat bani.

...like a village.

Confused expressions appeared around the room.

He pointed toward the map.

— Coal alag command.

Coal under separate command.

— Transport alag.

Transport separate.

— Security alag.

Security separate.

— Politics alag.

Politics separate.

Then his voice hardened.

— Isi wajah se bhai ke marwa dehal gail.

That is why Vikram was killed. The room became still. Very still.

Nobody argued. Because everyone knew he was right. Pratap had exploited gaps. Divisions. Lack of coordination. Internal weaknesses. The Empire's size had become its vulnerability.

Vardaan looked around the room. Slowly. Carefully. Making eye contact with every important figure. Then delivered the announcement.

— aj se purana bhtthi singh empire ke rajdhani banal.

The room exploded. Arguments. Questions. Shock. Disbelief. Some contractors objected immediately.

— Namumkin.

— bahute mahanga ho jail ba.

— hamni ke chetriy mukhyaly pahilhi hai se ba.

— local neta sob khtam ho jai..

Vardaan waited. Allowed the noise to continue. Allowed frustration to surface. Then simply raised his hand. The room immediately fell silent. Again. That silence. That obedience. It no longer felt unusual. It felt natural.

And that realization made him smile. Only slightly. But enough.

— Local neta hi to problem baa.

Regional autonomy is the problem. He pointed toward the map again.

— Ab se sab decision ek jagah se nikli.

From now on all decisions will come from one place.

— ek command.

— ek network.

— ek treasury.

— ek suraksa.

— ek Empire.

Nobody missed the implication. The Singh Empire was becoming a kingdom. And Vardaan was becoming its king.

From the rear of the chamber, Aarohi watched silently. Most people saw a leadership meeting. She saw something else. A transformation. The man standing before them barely resembled the scientist who once dreamed of stars. That version of Vardaan still existed somewhere. But every day it became harder to find.

After the meeting she found him alone near the furnace balcony. Looking out across the industrial skyline. Thousands of workers are moving below. Trucks. Machinery. Smoke stacks. Power.

— You enjoyed that right.

He smiled.

— A little.

— A little?

She crossed her arms.

— You looked like an emperor.

Vardaan laughed softly.

— Emperor?

Aarohi stepped beside him.

— Sacchi sacchi batao mujhe.

He remained silent. She continued.

— jab unhone baat karna band karke...

— jab woh log aapke faisle ka intezaar kar rahe the...

— jab sare aapki order ka palan kiya...

— Aapko kaisa mehsoos hua tha?

The answer arrived immediately.

Too soon.

— Great.

Aarohi looked away. Because that single word frightened her. Not because it was dishonest. Because it was honest.

Three days later, Vardaan announced another reform. The creation of an Inner Council. Five individuals. Direct access to him. Authority over every operational branch. Ramdeen. Security. Transport. Coal. Political Affairs. The move strengthened coordination dramatically. It also concentrated power. Every major decision now flowed through Bharat Furnace. Every major dispute. Every major contract. Every major conflict. Everything led back to Vardaan. Exactly as he intended. Not everyone accepted the new system. Especially the old guard. Several powerful contractors secretly met outside Dhanbad. They believed Vardaan was moving too quickly. Becoming too authoritarian. Too ambitious. Too dangerous.

One elderly operator slammed his glass against the table.

— Ee ladka pagal ho gaya baa.

This boy has gone mad. Another nodded.

— Vikram kabhu aisan na karat.

Vikram would never do this. A third added quietly.

— Humni ke support hata lete bani.

We should withdraw support.

The decision never reached completion. Because someone leaked the meeting. Twenty-four hours later, the same contractors received invitations. Not threats. Not summons. Invitations. To Bharat Furnace. The psychological effect was devastating. Because invitations from kings felt far more dangerous than threats from gangsters. The old contractors entered nervously. Expecting confrontation. Instead they found a banquet. Food. Hospitality. Respect. Everything appeared normal. Until Vardaan arrived. He greeted everyone warmly. Spoke politely. Listened patiently. Then finally stood.

— Gussa bani?

Are you angry? Nobody answered.

He smiled.

— I understand.

Then he slowly walked toward the furnace itself. The original furnace. The heart of the Empire. The place where Vairav and Jay Singh Bajwa built their first fortune.

— Ee furnace dekhat bani?

You see this furnace? The men nodded.

— Coal jab tak alag-alag tukda rahela...

As long as coal remains separate pieces...

—...tab tak keemat kam rahela.

...its value remains low.

Then he pointed toward the fire.

— But jab furnace me jaala...

But when it enters the furnace...

—...tab steel banta.

...it becomes steel.

Silence.

The message landed perfectly. You can remain separate and weak. Or unite and become powerful. By the end of the evening, every contractor pledged loyalty. Again. Some willingly. Some reluctantly. All effectively. Meanwhile, Aarohi's investigation uncovered another anomaly. One hidden inside old property records.A forgotten ownership structure from the early nineties. The document listed three trustees. Vairav Singh. Jay Singh Bajwa. And— Pratap Chauhan.

Aarohi stared at the page. Unable to process it. Trustee. Not an employee. Not an associate. Not a worker. Trustee. Which meant

Pratap had once possessed legal authority inside the Empire itself. The implications were enormous. She immediately carried the document to Vardaan. He studied it for several minutes. Without speaking. Without blinking. Then quietly asked:

— How many people know about this?

— Only us.

— Good.

His voice sounded colder than expected.

Because another realization had arrived. If Pratap once held authority— Then somebody had taken it away. And people rarely start wars because of money. They start wars because of betrayal. Long after everyone left, Vardaan remained inside the furnace chamber. Alone. The old tape recorder sat before him. Vikram's unfinished message. The photographs. The trustee records. The erased history. Everything scattered across the table. Outside, Bharat Furnace glowed against the darkness. Like a kingdom made of fire. A kingdom that now belonged entirely to him. For a moment he imagined the future. Pratap defeated. Jay Singh Bajwa exposed. The Empire united. His enemies were destroyed. His legacy was secured. And for the first time— The dream no longer frightened him. It excited him.

Far away, inside the abandoned church, Pratap Chauhan sat before a faded photograph of Vikram. A storm raged outside. Lightning illuminated his face.

One of his men entered.

— Naya khabar.

New information.

Pratap looked up.

— What?

The lieutenant answered quietly.

— Vardaan officially took control of everything.

A long silence followed. Then Pratap looked toward Vikram's photograph. And whispered something nobody else heard.

— Exactly as they wanted.

The lieutenant frowned.

— Who?

Pratap never answered. Outside, thunder rolled across the coal belt. And somewhere in that darkness, a man named Jay Singh Bajwa smiled. Because every step Vardaan took toward the throne — Brought him closer to the trap waiting at the end of it.

CHAPTER EIGHTEEN

THE NIGHT OF ASHES

Coal Belt Region, October, 2019

Empires rarely collapse in a single day. They bleed first. Slowly. Quietly. One wound at a time. One betrayal at a time. One fire at a time. And on a humid June night, as dark clouds gathered over the coal belt, Pratap Chauhan decided it was time to make the Singh Empire bleed.

Bharat Furnace

The first call came at 10:17 PM. A transport depot near Bokaro was burning. At first, nobody panicked. Depots burned occasionally. Insurance fraud. Local disputes. Accidents. Nothing unusual. Then a second call arrived. A coal stockyard near Giridih. Burning. Then a third. Then a fourth. Then a sixth. By 11 PM, the crisis room inside Bharat Furnace resembled a war command center. Maps covered the walls. Phones rang continuously. Security officers shouted coordinates. Contractors demanded answers. Fear spreads faster than information. Ramdeen looked toward Vardaan.

— Ee normal na baa.

This isn't normal. Vardaan already knew. The attacks were too synchronized. Too precise. Too organized. Pratap had finally moved.

By midnight, reports became catastrophic. Three transport routes were blocked. Two warehouses were destroyed. Four district coordinators are missing. Multiple fuel depots under attack. Entire villages abandoning contested zones. It wasn't gang warfare. It was economic warfare. The objective wasn't territory. The objective was paralysis.

Vardaan stood before the giant map of the Empire. Red lights continued appearing. One after another. Like wounds. Fresh wounds. The pattern slowly emerged. Every target occupied a strategic location. Every target connected to recently centralized operations. Every target strengthened the Empire. Pratap wasn't attacking randomly. He was dismantling Vardaan's reforms. Piece by piece.

Then the worst news arrived. A frightened contractor entered the room. Covered in dust. Shaking. Barely able to speak.

— Malik...

His voice cracked.

— Dumri mine...

Vardaan looked up immediately.

— What happened?

The man swallowed. Then whispered:

— They surrendered.

The room froze. Surrender. The word itself felt impossible. The Singh Empire did not surrender. Not under Vairav. Not under Vikram. Not under anyone. Yet tonight it happened.

Another message arrived. Then another. And another. Three additional territories declared neutrality. Two switched allegiance entirely. The infection was spreading.

For the first time since becoming king, Vardaan felt something he hadn't experienced in months. Fear. Not fear of death. Fear of losing. Fear that everything he had built could disappear.

By morning, thousands of workers were fleeing contested regions. Entire families packed belongings onto trucks. Roads became crowded with frightened people. Children. Miners. Drivers. Farmers. Everyone is moving away from uncertainty. Away from violence. Away from war.

News channels arrived quickly. Drone footage captured long lines of displaced workers. Headlines spread across television screens.

COAL BELT DESCENDS INTO CHAOS
SINGH EMPIRE LOSING CONTROL?
WHO REALLY RULES THE REGION?

For Pratap, the images were more valuable than any military victory. Because power depended on perception. And perception was changing.

While the Empire burned, Aarohi continued searching through the Ghost Files. Because something bothered her. Deeply.

Pratap's attacks felt personal. Too personal. Almost intimate. As though he knew exactly how the Empire functioned. Exactly where weaknesses existed. Exactly where to strike. Which meant one thing. He wasn't learning about the Empire. He remembered it.

Inside another forgotten archive box, she discovered a collection of planning maps from nearly thirty years earlier. Infrastructure plans. Future transport routes. Storage facilities. Mine expansion proposals.

Several documents carried familiar signatures. Vairav Singh. Jay Singh Bajwa. And— Pratap Chauhan. Aarohi stared at the signatures. Then at the dates. Then back at the signatures.

Pratap had helped design parts of the Empire. Years before becoming its enemy. The realization chilled her. Because it explained everything. The attacks. The precision. The strategy. The accuracy. Pratap wasn't attacking from outside. He was attacking a house he once helped build.

The most devastating battle of the campaign began the following night. A massive coal storage complex outside Dhanbad. One of the largest in the region. Critical to transport operations. Critical to revenue. Critical to survival.

Around midnight, Pratap's forces surrounded it. Not hundreds. Thousands. Armed men emerging from darkness. Motorcycles. Pickup trucks. Heavy vehicles. An army disguised as a gang. Inside Bharat Furnace, intelligence reached Vardaan almost immediately.

The advisers urged caution. They wanted reinforcements. Planning. Coordination. Time. Vardaan refused.

The old scientist might have listened. The new king did not.

— Gaari Ready karo.

Ramdeen frowned.

— Malik—

— Gaari Ready karo.

No discussion. No debate. No compromise.

An hour later, Vardaan led the response personally. Convoys thundered across highways. Headlights cutting through darkness. Workers lined roads watching them pass. Some folded hands. Some shouted blessings. Some simply stared. Because stories are spreading now. Stories bigger than truth. Bigger than reality.

The Coal Belt King was coming.

The coal yard resembled a war zone. Explosions illuminated the night. Coal mountains burned like volcanic hills. Smoke covered the sky. Gunfire echoed endlessly. Vardaan arrived directly into chaos. Not behind it. Not after it. Into it. His men established positions immediately. Counterattacks began. Vehicles crashed through barricades. Bullets shattered floodlights. Darkness swallowed entire sections of the battlefield.

For hours the fight continued. Brutal. Relentless. Unforgiving. Then something changed. Vardaan stopped directing from the rear. Stopped observing. Stopped calculating. Instead, he moved forward. Toward the front lines. Toward the violence. Toward the fire.

Ramdeen shouted after him.

— Malik!

Too late. Vardaan was already advancing.

Something had awakened inside him. Something born from grief. Fed by responsibility. Strengthened by power.

And for the first time— He enjoyed it.

Not the killing. Not the blood. The control. The certainty. The feeling that every man around him moved because he commanded it.

The battlefield responded to his presence. Morale surged. Men fought harder. Workers refused retreat. Drivers joined defenses. Even wounded guards returned to positions. Because kings inspired. And kings terrified. Vardaan was becoming both.

By dawn, the siege ended. Pratap's forces withdrew. The coal yard survived. Barely. Hundreds injured. Dozens dead. Millions lost. Yet strategically— The Empire held.

The workers gathered as sunlight rose through smoke-covered skies. Thousands of them. Miners. Drivers. Contractors. Families. They looked at Vardaan standing atop a burned loading platform. Covered in soot. Covered in exhaustion. Still standing. Then somebody began clapping. Another joined. Then another. Then hundreds. Then thousands. Soon the entire yard echoed with applause. Not for victory. For survival.

And standing above them all, Vardaan felt something dangerous again. That same feeling. Stronger now. More seductive. More intoxicating. Not gratitude. Not pride. Destiny.

Far away, inside the abandoned church, Pratap listened to casualty reports. The lieutenant seemed confused.

— We lost ground.

Pratap nodded.

— The coal yard survived.

Again, he nodded. The lieutenant finally exploded.

— Toh phir ee sab ka fayda?

Then what was the point of all this?

Pratap slowly stood. Walked toward an old photograph resting beside a candle. Young Vikram. Young Pratap. Side by side. Then quietly answered.

— Ab woh Raja ban raha hai.

Now he is becoming a king. The lieutenant frowned. Pratap's eyes remained fixed on the photograph.

— Aur har raja...

A long pause.

— ...kabhi na kabhi chuuk karta hi hai .

Outside, thunder rolled across the horizon. And somewhere beyond the coal belt, beyond the highways, beyond the burning yards, a man named Jay Singh Bajwa watched events unfold exactly as planned. Because every victory Vardaan achieved was pushing him toward the same destination. The Furnace Throne. The throne that had already destroyed one generation. The throne that had already destroyed another. And soon— Would demand its next sacrifice.

CHAPTER NINETEEN

The Devil In White

An Abandoned Mission Church, Near The Bengal Border, October, 2020

For nearly a year, the coal belt had burned. Mines. Roads. Warehouses. Villages. Families. Everything caught in the war between two men. Vardaan Singh. Pratap Chauhan. King and usurper. Brother and betrayer. Hunter and hunted. Yet despite countless battles, they had never spoken. Not once. Not since Vikram's death. Not face-to-face. Not as men. Only through bullets. Only through blood. Until now.

The proposal arrived unexpectedly. A handwritten message. Delivered by an elderly priest. No threats. No demands. Only a location. And a sentence.

"If you truly want answers, come alone." Signed. *Pratap.*

At Bharat Furnace, every adviser opposed it. Every single one.

— Ee u logo ka shazish baa."

It's their trap.

— Mat jaiye Malik.

Don't go.

— Hum log Pratap ke location trace kar sakat bani.

We can track him instead. Ramdeen remained silent longer than everyone else. Then finally said:

— Malik...

Vardaan looked toward him. The old caretaker sighed.

— Kabhi-kabhi sach jaan ke khatir jaan ke risk lewa padela.

Sometimes, to know the truth, you must risk your life. The room became silent. Because everyone knew why Vardaan would go. Not for strategy. Not for advantage. Not even for revenge. For Vikram.

The mission church stood forgotten by time. Built during colonial years. Abandoned decades ago. Half consumed by forest. Half consumed by memory. Rain clouds gathered overhead. The evening sky glowed dark blue. Thunder rumbled in the distance.

Vardaan arrived alone. Exactly as requested. No convoy. No guards. No backup.

Inside the church, hundreds of candles burned. Their light danced against ancient stone walls. The atmosphere felt strangely peaceful. Almost sacred. And sitting near the altar— Dressed entirely in white— Waited Pratap Chauhan.

For several seconds neither man moved. Neither spoke. Neither looked away. Two lives. Two destinies. Two versions of the same tragedy.

Finally Pratap stood. Older now. Harder now. The years had carved suffering into his face. Yet there was something unexpected in his eyes. Not hatred. Not fear. Not arrogance. Sadness. Deep sadness.

— Baith ja.

Sit.

Vardaan remained standing.

— Humra bhai ke kahein marla?

Why did you kill my brother?

No greeting. No introduction. Straight to the wound.

Pratap nodded slowly. As if he expected nothing less. Then quietly answered.

— Ee sawal poochhe khatir hi tu aail baa.

That's why you've come. The church fell silent again. Finally Vardaan sat. Across from the man he had spent a year trying to destroy.

For a long moment, Pratap stared at a candle flame. Almost mesmerized by it.

Then he spoke.

— Yaad baa tohra bachpan?

Do you remember your childhood?

Vardaan frowned.

"Kya?"

Pratap smiled faintly.

— Humra yaad baa.

I remember mine. His eyes drifted toward the stained-glass window. Toward another time. Another life.

— Hum anath rahni.

I was an orphan.

— Tohra baap Vairav Singh humke ghar le aail rahin.

Your Father Vairav Singh brought me home. The words hit Vardaan like a punch.

Not because they were surprising. Because they confirmed everything. The photographs. The records. The trustee documents.

Pratap continued.

— Log naukar bolat rahin.

People called me a servant.

A small smile appeared.

— Vikram kabhu na.

Vikram never did.

For the first time during the meeting, emotion entered his voice. Real emotion.

— Humni ek saath school gaili.

We went to school together.

— Ek saath pitai khaili.

We got beaten together.

— Ek saath sapna dekhlili.

We dreamed together.

A pause. Then quietly:

— Vikram sirf tohra na, hamaar bhi bhai rahal.

Vikram was not only yours, but also my brother.

The words echoed through the church. Vardaan felt something inside him shift. Not forgiveness. Never forgiveness. But confusion. Because liars rarely spoke with grief.

Rain began falling outside. Heavy. Relentless. The church roof echoed with its rhythm. Pratap poured tea into two metal cups. Placed one before Vardaan. Neither touched it.

Then came the question.

— Tohra lagela Vikram ke maut se sabse jyada fayda kehu ke bhayil?"

Who benefited most from Vikram's death?

— Tu.

You.

Pratap laughed. A bitter laugh.

— Galat.

Wrong. Then leaned forward.

— Hum hi Vikram ke marli.

I killed Vikram.

Silence. Absolute silence. Pratap didn't look away. Didn't justify it. Didn't soften it. Simply accepted it. *"I killed him."* Vardaan's fists tightened. Every instinct screamed to attack. To kill. To finish this. Yet something stopped him. Because Pratap wasn't defending himself. He was confessing.

Pratap reached inside his coat. Slowly. Carefully. Vardaan tensed. Instead of a weapon, Pratap removed a photograph. Old. Faded. Worn.

He slid it across the table. Vardaan looked down. And froze.

The photograph showed: Vairav Singh. Jay Singh Bajwa. Young Vikram. Young Pratap. And— A much younger Vardaan. All standing together. Smiling. Like family.

The image felt impossible. Because nowhere in his memories did Pratap exist. Someone had erased him. Deliberately.

Pratap's expression darkened.

— Tohra lagela ee sab hum plan kaili?

You think I planned all this? He shook his head.

— Nahi.

No.

Then for the first time— The name emerged. The name that had haunted every chapter of the story. Every tragedy. Every mystery.

Every wound.

— Jay Singh Bajwa.

The church seemed to grow colder. Vardaan remained silent. Pratap continued.

— u hamra ke satta sikhavle.

— u hamra ke bafadaari sikhavle.

— u hamra ke nafrat sikhavle.

A pause. Then:

— aau ek din ke..."

His voice cracked.

—...u hamra ke dhokebaazi sikhavle.

Lightning illuminated the church. For a brief moment, both men appeared like figures inside a myth. Pratap stood. Walked toward the altar.

—Tu jaanne chahat baa na...

You want to know...

—...kaise Vikram maral?

...how Vikram died?

Vardaan rose immediately.

— Bol.

Speak.

Pratap stared at the cross hanging above the altar. Then whispered:

— Vikram ke maut uska shaadi par na bhayil.

Vikram's death didn't begin on his wedding day. The words lingered.

— Vikram ke maut saalon pahile shuru ho chuki rahal.

His death began years earlier.

Another revelation. Another wound. Another mystery. Pratap turned toward him.

For the first time, genuine fear appeared in his eyes. Not fear of Vardaan. Fear of memory. Fear of truth. Fear of Jay Singh Bajwa.

— Uss din bass tohar bhai ke hum maarli.

I just killed your brother on that day. Then came the sentence that changed everything.

— But kahani oo na baa je tu sochat baa.

But the story isn't what you think it is.

Before Vardaan could respond, Pratap removed another object. A cassette tape. Identical to the one found inside Vikram's box. Vardaan's eyes widened. Pratap placed it on the table.

— He recorded two.

The church became silent.

— Ek tohra khatir.

One for you.

— Ek humra khatir.

One for me.

The implications were staggering. Vikram knew. Before his death. He knew something. Something involving Pratap. Something involving Jay Singh Bajwa. Something large enough to destroy an empire.

The rain finally began slowing. The meeting had lasted nearly three hours. Yet Vardaan left with more questions than answers. Pratap remained inside the church. Standing before the altar. Alone. As Vardaan reached the doorway, he stopped. Without turning around. One final question.

— Kahe?

Why?

Pratap understood immediately. Why kill Vikram? Why betray family? Why start the war? A long silence followed. Then came the answer. Soft. Broken. Almost inaudible.

— kahe ki kuchh karja virasat mein milta hai.

Vardaan turned. But Pratap was already walking back into darkness.

And for the first time since Vikram's death— Vardaan wondered if the man he hated most in the world was also one of its victims. Outside, storm clouds drifted across the coal belt.

Far away, inside a luxurious estate hidden from public view, Jay Singh Bajwa sat alone with a glass of whisky. A servant entered quietly.

— mulakat bhail.

The meeting happened.

Bajwa smiled. A slow smile. The smile of a man watching pieces move exactly as intended. Because he knew something neither Vardaan nor Pratap understood yet. The truth had finally begun surfacing. And truth— was far more dangerous than war.

CHAPTER TWENTY

THE BROTHER HE CHOSE

Bharat Furnace, November-December, 2019

The dead leave behind many things. Photographs. Letters. Property. Memories. But sometimes they leave behind questions. Questions that refuse to die.

Three nights had passed since Vardaan's meeting with Pratap Chauhan. Three sleepless nights. Three nights spent listening to Vikram's unfinished cassette. Again. And again. And again. Searching for something hidden between words. Some clues. Some warning. Some answers. Yet every time the tape ended at the same place. Abruptly. Incomplete. Like a life interrupted.

The second cassette now sat beside it. Pratap's cassette. Vikram's message meant for another man. Another brother. Another victim.

Aarohi sat across from him inside Vikram's old office. The room smelled of dust, old paper, and late-night exhaustion. Files covered every surface. Photographs. Property records. Trust deeds. School documents. The Ghost Files continued growing.

— Listen to this.

Aarohi inserted another tape into the recorder. Static crackled. Then voices emerged. Children's voices. Laughter. Someone recording a school event decades earlier.

Vardaan frowned.

— What is this?

Aarohi smiled faintly.

— Ranchi Boarding School archives.

Then she pressed pause.

— Listen carefully.

The tape resumed. A teacher announced race results. Students cheered. Footsteps. Applause. Then a familiar voice. Young. Energetic. Alive. Vikram Singh.

Vardaan froze. The voice continued.

— Pratap! Jaldi aa!

Pratap! Hurry up!

Another boy laughed loudly.

— Ruk na, pagal!

Wait, idiot!

The recording ended. Silence filled the room. For several seconds Vardaan couldn't speak. Because for the first time he wasn't hearing about Vikram and Pratap. He was hearing them. Together. Like brothers.

The past arrived gradually. Like old smoke returning from forgotten fires. Aarohi had spent days reconstructing records. School reports. Yearbooks. Archived photographs. Personal testimonies. The picture becoming visible was unlike anything Vardaan expected.

At school, Vikram Singh wasn't feared. He wasn't respected because of power. He wasn't heir to an empire. He was simply Vikram. And Pratap was never far away. One photograph showed them fighting over a cricket bat. Another showed them standing punishment outside a classroom. Another captured them sleeping on the same train berth during a school trip.

Brothers. In every way except blood.

An elderly retired teacher agreed to speak through a video call. Professor Harinarayan Jha. Eighty-one years old. Sharp memory. Sharp tongue. The old teacher laughed when shown their photographs.

— Arre ee dono?

These two?

— Hamaar school ke sabse bada musibat.

The biggest troublemakers in my school.

Aarohi smiled.

— Kaise thein woh dono?

The professor leaned back.

— Vikram sabka neta bane firta rahal."

Vikram was a protector.

— Aur Pratap fighter"

Pratap was a fighter.

Then came a statement that stayed with Vardaan.

— Ek dusra ke bina adhura.

Incomplete without each other.

Later that evening, Vardaan sat alone with the photographs. A strange feeling grew inside him. Not sympathy. Not forgiveness. Something else. Grief. Because every new discovery forced him to lose Vikram again. And again. And again. Not only had Vikram died. An entire life had died with him. An entire future. A future that once included Pratap.

Among the recovered records was one particular report. A disciplinary report from 1993.

The document described a violent fight involving six senior students. One student was nearly hospitalized. Several suspensions recommended. At the bottom of the report appeared two names. Vikram Singh. Pratap Chauhan. Aarohi tracked down another witness. Former student Mahesh Tiwari. Now a retired bank manager.

His memory remained surprisingly clear.

— Hum sab dekhal.

I saw everything.

— Kya hua tha?" Aarohi asked.

Mahesh laughed.

— Vikram ke caste aur family ke naam pe taunt karat rahin kuch senior log.

Some seniors were mocking Vikram's family and background.

"Pratap sun li."

Pratap heard it.

The old man smiled.

— Phir narak khul gail.

Then hell opened.

According to every witness, Pratap attacked six boys alone. Not because they insulted him. Because they insulted Vikram. The fight became legendary. Both boys were suspended. Both punished. Both refused to blame each other. Together. Always together.

Yet buried within the records, Aarohi discovered something else. Something darker.

A letter. Written by Vikram. Never sent. The paper had yellowed with age. The handwriting is unmistakable. The letter addressed only one person. Pratap.

Vardaan read it slowly.

— Tu hamaar bhai baa.

You are my brother.

— Lekin kuch log chahat baa ki humni alag ho jai.

But some people want us separated.

— Hum samajhat na ki kahein.

I don't understand why.

— Lekin sambhal ke rah.

Be careful.

No signature. No explanation. No context. Only warning. The date stunned everyone. 1995. Nearly twenty-five years earlier. Meaning the division between Vikram and Pratap had begun long before Vairav's death. Long before the war. Long before betrayal. Someone had been working on it for decades.

That night Vardaan visited Ramdeen. The old caretaker sat beneath a neem tree outside the furnace complex. Drinking tea. Watching workers change shifts. Without introduction, Vardaan handed him the letter. Ramdeen read it. Then closed his eyes. A long silence followed. Finally:

— Hum sochle rahni ee din kabhu na aayi.

I hoped this day would never come. Vardaan sat beside him.

— Ka hua?

Ramdeen didn't answer immediately. Instead he looked toward the dark industrial skyline. Then spoke.

— jab vairav singh aau jayasingh bajva e sab bnvle...

His voice softened.

—...u log apna mooran ke ek sang hi badha kile.

Vardaan listened carefully.

— Ek ghar.

— ek table.

— Ek hi tiwhaar.

Then:

— Ek sapne.

The statement hit harder than expected. Because suddenly the entire story transformed. This wasn't merely gang warfare. This wasn't a conflict between enemies. It was a civil war. A family destroying itself.

Ramdeen eventually stood. Old bones protesting every movement. Then he said something that changed the chapter.

— Sab kuch badalal jab Jay Singh Bajwa badlal.

Everything changed when Jay Singh Bajwa changed. The air seemed to grow heavier. Vardaan remained silent. Ramdeen continued.

— Pehle oo Vairav ke jaan rahal.

Earlier he would have died for Vairav.

— Phir ek din...

Then one day...

The old caretaker stopped. As if remembering something painful.

—...oo power ke pyaar mein pad gail.

He fell in love with power. The words lingered. Not money. Not land. Not revenge. Power. The most addictive thing in the world.

Near midnight, Vardaan finally listened to Pratap's cassette. Alone. No advisers. No Aarohi. No interruptions. Only darkness. And Vikram's voice. Static. Then silence. Then—

— Pratap...

A pause.

— If you're hearing this...

Another pause.

—...tab ya t hamni ke pahilhi se mar gail ja...

The tape hissed.

—...aau uu aakhirkar safal ho gail ba.

Vardaan sat upright instantly. Every nerve in his body tightened. The message continued.

— Hum sach samajh gail bani.

I finally understand the truth.

— Bahut der se.

Too late. Static swallowed part of the recording. Then came the final audible sentence. The sentence that shattered everything.

— Humni ke ladai kabhu hamni ke rahal hi na.

This war was never ours. The tape ended. Abruptly. Again. Silence. Absolute silence.

Outside, dawn slowly approached. The coal belt slept uneasily. Workers prepared for another day. Contractors prepared for another battle. Politicians prepared for another lie. And somewhere in the darkness, Jay Singh Bajwa sat awake. Reading intelligence reports. Monitoring movements. Watching the Empire consume itself. Exactly as it had for decades.

Because while Vardaan and Pratap searched for answers— Bajwa already knew them. Every answer. Every secret. Every betrayal. And soon— The first true crack in the foundation of the Singh Empire would finally be revealed. The crack that began not with Vikram. Not with Pratap. Not with Vardaan. But with two brothers. Vairav Singh. And Jay Singh Bajwa.

CHAPTER TWENTY-ONE

BLOOD BROTHERS

Southern Bihar Coal Belt, Winter, 1981

Long before the Empire. Long before Bharat Furnace. Long before Vikram. Long before Vardaan. Before coal became power. Before politics became business. Before betrayal became inheritance. There were only two brothers. And a promise.

The winter of 1981 was brutal. The villages around the coal belt survived one season at a time. One harvest. One wage. One meal. Most families owned nothing. The lucky ones owned land. The unlucky ones worked it. The cursed ones worked inside illegal mines.

Among the cursed were two young men. Vairav Singh. Jay Singh Bajwa. They were not brothers by blood. But everyone believed they were. Because wherever one appeared, the other followed.

The people called them: *"Do Jaan, Ek Talwar - Two souls. One sword"*.

At dawn they entered abandoned mine shafts. At night they guarded villages from bandits. In between they hauled coal on their backs like beasts of burden. The coal contractors exploited everyone. Police took bribes. Politicians ignored complaints. Criminal gangs ruled roads. The poor suffered. The powerful prospered. One evening, after fourteen hours inside a collapsing mine tunnel, Jay threw his shovel aside.

— Ee zindagi na chale.

This life cannot continue. Vairav laughed.

— Toh ka kari?

Then what should we do?

Jay looked toward the distant horizon. Toward the glowing chimneys of industrial plants. Toward wealth. Toward power.

— Ek din humni sab kuch kharid leba.

One day we'll own all of this.

Vairav shook his head.

— Humni ke roti ke paisa na baa.

We don't even have money for bread.

Jay smiled.

— Abhi na.

Not yet.

Then quietly:

— Par ek din.

One day.

That day arrived sooner than expected. A local gang led by Bhola Thakur controlled illegal coal extraction in the region. Workers were beaten. Women harassed. Children forced into labor. Nobody resisted. Because resistance meant death. Until Bhola's men made a mistake. They attacked Vairav's village. A twelve-year-old boy lost an eye. An old farmer was beaten nearly to death. Three families abandoned their homes.

The entire village gathered beneath a banyan tree. Fear covered every face. One elder sighed.

— Kuch na ho sakela.

Nothing can be done.

Then Jay stood.

— Ho sakela.

Something can be done.

The crowd turned. The elder laughed bitterly.

— Ka?

What?

Jay pointed toward the forest.

— Larai.

Fight.

The villagers stared. As if he had suggested madness. Perhaps he had.

That night, thirty villagers followed Vairav and Jay into the forest. Most carried sticks. Some carried farming tools. A few carried rusted rifles. Bhola Thakur commanded nearly two hundred armed men. The odds were absurd. Vairav noticed immediately.

— Jay...

—Haan?

Yes?

— Hum mar jaib.

We're going to die. Jay laughed loudly.

— Tab toh Bhola ke saath mil jai.

Then we'll get company in death.

Even Vairav laughed. Minutes later the battle began. The forest erupted. Gunshots. Screams. Chaos. Fire. For three hours villagers fought like cornered animals. Not for territory. Not for profit. For dignity. When dawn arrived, Bhola Thakur's gang no longer existed. The victory became a legend. Not because they won. Because they should not have.

Stories spread quickly. Village to village. Mine to mine. District to district. *"Two teenage brothers had defeated a king"*.

Opportunity followed reputation. Miners began approaching them. Transporters sought protection. Villages requested security. Contractors offered partnerships.

For the first time in their lives— Money arrived. Not much. But enough. Together they purchased a broken brick kiln. Then another. Then a transport truck. Then another. Each success created another. Each victory strengthened loyalty. Within five years they controlled multiple coal routes. Several brick industries. Dozens of villages. And unlike most local strongmen— They shared profits. Workers loved them. Villagers protected them. Criminals feared them. Legends grew. Some called them kings. Vairav hated the title. Jay loved it.

Bharat Furnace

The dream truly began in 1989. An abandoned industrial site outside Dhanbad. Bankrupt. Collapsed. Worthless. Everyone called it a mistake. Jay called it destiny. Standing before the rusted structure, he spread his arms dramatically.

— Dekhat bada?

See this?

Vairav laughed.

— Kachra.

Junk.

Jay shook his head.

— Empire.

The furnace would eventually become Bharat Furnace. The heart of everything. The birthplace of the Singh Empire.

Then came the woman. Every empire eventually reaches a turning point. For Jay Singh Bajwa— Her name was Savitri. She arrived as a school volunteer. Educated. Strong-willed. Fearless. Unlike others, she wasn't impressed by power. When Jay tried boasting about future ambitions, she laughed.

— Power se character na banta.

Power doesn't build character.

Jay spent days thinking about those words. And weeks thinking about her. For the first time in his life— The ambitious young dreamer fell in love. Deeply. Hopelessly. Completely. But fate had other plans. Because Savitri loved someone else. Vairav Singh. Months later the village celebrated Holi. The largest gathering of the year. Music. Food. Bhaang. Color. Joy. The entire region attended. Including Jay. Including Savitri. Including Vairav. And during the celebration— Vairav proposed. Before everyone. The crowd erupted. Cheers. Laughter. Blessings. Savitri said yes. The entire village celebrated. Everyone. Except for one man. Jay Singh Bajwa. Standing alone beneath a neem tree. Watching. Smiling. Clapping. Pretending. While something inside him quietly broke.

Later that night, after the celebration ended, Jay sat beside Bharat Furnace. Alone. Drinking. Thinking. Vairav eventually found him.

— Bhai.

Brother.

Jay looked up.

— Haan?

Vairav smiled.

— Hum aj bohot khush bani."

Today I'm very happy.

Jay forced a smile.

— Hum bhi.

Me too.

The lie tasted bitter. He gulps his glass at once, perhaps to soothe the bitterness a bit. For several moments neither spoke. Then Vairav placed a hand on his shoulder.

— Sab kuch humni ke baa.

Everything belongs to us.

Jay nodded. But his eyes drifted toward the furnace. Toward the growing empire. Toward the future. And for the first time— He wondered if everything truly belonged to both of them. Or if one man always received more. More respect. More love. More loyalty. More credit. More everything. The thought lasted only seconds. Then it disappeared. But some seeds do not need much time. Only fertile soil. And envy had finally found its soil.

Present Day, Bharat Furnace

Ramdeen's voice faded. The story ended. The old caretaker looked exhausted. Vardaan sat silently. Processing everything. The rise. The brotherhood. The dream. The love. The first crack. Because now he understood something terrifying. Jay Singh Bajwa wasn't born evil. He became evil. Slowly. Gradually. Over decades. Which made him infinitely more dangerous. Outside, Bharat Furnace glowed against the night sky. A kingdom built by two brothers. A kingdom that would eventually destroy three generations. And somewhere far away, Jay Singh Bajwa stood before a mirror. An old photograph resting nearby. The same photograph from the early days. Him. Vairav. Savitri. Smiling. Dreaming. Believing.

He picked up the photograph. Stared at it. Then quietly whispered:

— Sab kuch wahi din se shuru bhail.

Everything began that day. The day Savitri chose Vairav. The day love became jealousy. The day brotherhood began dying.

CHAPTER TWENTY-TWO

THE CROWN AND THE WOUND

Bharat Furnace, March, 2020

The coal belt had never sounded this quiet. No roaring truck convoys. No furnace whistles before dawn. No drunken songs from labor camps. Only sirens, loudspeakers, and the endless announcement repeated across villages and highways:

— *Ghar se bahar mat nikliye. Mask pehniye. Do gaz ki doori banaye rakhiye.*

India was under lockdown. The highways that once carried the Singh Empire's lifeblood now looked abandoned. Trucks stood parked for miles like rusting animals waiting for permission to move again. And inside Bharat Furnace, the Empire was bleeding. Revenue had collapsed by more than half in six weeks. Mines operated with skeletal crews. Transport routes required government passes. Police checkpoints multiplied across state borders. But the worst problem was not economic. It was human. Thousands of migrant workers were stranded across the coal belt with no wages, no transport, and no certainty of survival.

The emergency council meeting lasted until past midnight. Contractors demanded shutdowns. Accountants demanded cost-cutting. Security chiefs warned that armed gangs were looting supply warehouses. Ramdeen placed a file before Vardaan.

— agar hamni ka mjdurn ke paisa det rahin ja, t du mahina ka bheetr dene ke liye aur kuchhu nahi bachega.

Another adviser added:

— Malik, yeh khairat ka waqt nahi hai.

This is not the time for charity.

Vardaan looked around the room. Faces tired. Anxious. Calculating survival. Then he stood.

— Mine bandh ho sakta hai.

Mines can shut down.

— Transport ruk sakta hai.

Transport can stop.

— Lekin log bhookhe nahi marenge.

But our people will not die hungry. The room went silent. He continued:

— Ration camps kholiye.

Open ration camps.

— Dawa-daaru ka supply secure kariye.

Secure medicine supplies.

— Aur jo mazdoor ghar jaana chahta hai, uske liye gaadi niklegi.

And any worker who wants to return home will be given transport. Several contractors protested immediately.

— Asamvaab!

— Loss aur badhega!

— Government ka kaam hum kyon karein?

Why should we do the government's job?

Vardaan's voice hardened.

— Kyunki government abhi humse kam kaam kar rahi hai.

Because the government is doing less than we are right now. No one spoke after that.

Within days, Bharat Furnace transformed into something nobody expected. The main transport yard became a relief center. Coal warehouses stored food sacks instead of cargo. Security vehicles delivered oxygen cylinders and medicines to remote villages. Women cooked in giant community kitchens. Doctors volunteered under Empire protection. Workers who once feared the Singh family now stood in line for help from it. And every relief packet carried the same stamp: *BHARAT FURNACE RELIEF NETWORK*. Rumors spread faster than official news. Some called Vardaan a criminal buying loyalty. Others called him a savior. Most people simply called him the only man helping them.

Aarohi watched the transformation uneasily. One evening she found Vardaan distributing food near an old railway siding. Children crowded around him. Miners folded their hands in gratitude. He looked exhausted. But alive in a strange new way. Later, when the crowd dispersed, she spoke quietly.

— You know what they're calling you now?

He smiled tiredly.

— I'm too afraid to ask.

— Ration Raja.

The Ration King. Vardaan laughed. Then the laughter faded.

— Funny thing is... I'm not doing this for reputation.

Aarohi studied him carefully.

— Then why?

He looked toward the campfires where workers were eating dinner.

— Because if these people collapse, the Empire deserves to collapse with them.

For a moment, she saw the old Vardaan again. The scientist. The human being. Not the king.

Elsewhere, Pratap Chauhan saw the pandemic differently. Where others saw tragedy, he saw leverage. Government restrictions created shortages overnight. Medicines disappeared from pharmacies. Oxygen cylinders became currency. Movement permits became gold. And Pratap controlled the roads nobody officially admitted existed. Illegal transport corridors through forests and mining trails. His men began running: *Black-market medicine shipments. Fake sanitizer and PPE supplies. Interstate transport for desperate migrants. Oxygen cylinder diversion from hospitals. Cash-for-permit operations.* The profits were enormous. But more importantly, dependence was growing. Fear makes people obedient.

The first direct clash came in late April. A Singh relief convoy carrying oxygen cylinders toward a district hospital disappeared near Topchanchi. By the time Vardaan's men traced it, the cylinders had already entered Pratap-controlled distribution channels. Vardaan arrived at the checkpoint personally. Again. The local officer avoided eye contact.

— Sir... paperwork issue tha.

There was a paperwork issue. Vardaan walked past him. Inside a warehouse, he found rows of oxygen cylinders stacked beside cartons of counterfeit medicines. Workers stood trembling. One finally whispered:

— Pratap ke log le gaye aadha maal.

Pratap's men took half the shipment. Vardaan stared at the cylinders for a long moment. Then quietly said:

— Godam to seal kar do.

He turned to Ramdeen.

— har silendr pahile hasptal jala. kavno bajar bikri na hokhe.

And then, colder:

— Jo nakli dawai bana raha hai, usko dhoondo.

Find whoever is making the fake medicines.

That night, something unprecedented happened. Instead of issuing threats through intermediaries, Vardaan recorded a public message from Bharat Furnace. The video spread across WhatsApp groups and local news channels. He stood alone in the furnace hall, wearing a plain mask and no jewelry.

— Ee samay jang ka nahi, insaaniyat ka hai.

— Lekin jo log bimari se paisa kama rahe hain... jo oxygen aur dawa chura rahe hain... unke liye hum maafi nahi rakhenge.

— Coal Belt mein ek hi rule chalega — zaruratmand ko madad milegi, aur lootne wale ko saza.

The message changed the atmosphere overnight. Workers began reporting black-market operations anonymously. Truck drivers shared hidden routes. Local doctors leaked names of corrupt suppliers. For the first time, information started flowing toward the

Empire instead of away from it.

While the region battled the pandemic, Aarohi continued untangling the past. Government archives were partially closed due to lockdown, forcing her to rely on scanned records, retired clerks, and private collections. Inside an old district registry file, she found something explosive. A land-transfer document from 2001.

The property was officially sold by a shell company to a transport cooperative. But the witnesses listed on the deed included: *Jay Singh Bajwa, Mahender Suri, Pratap Chauhan.* And the location of the property made her blood run cold. It was the same forest corridor now used by Pratap's illegal lockdown transport network. This wasn't improvisation. The route had been secured two decades earlier. Jay Singh Bajwa had prepared for hidden logistics long before the pandemic, long before Vikram's death, long before the current war. A shadow infrastructure beneath the official Empire.

In Late April and early May, COVID cases surged through the mining districts. One district hospital near Bokaro nearly collapsed after oxygen supplies ran dry. Panic spread across the town. Relatives screamed outside wards. Doctors threatened resignation. Ambulances lined the road. At 2:30 a.m., a convoy of Bharat Furnace trucks arrived carrying emergency cylinders. Vardaan stepped out first. Exhausted nurses began crying openly. A junior doctor grabbed his arm.

— Agar yeh aadha ghanta aur late hota na... ward khali ho jata.

If this had arrived half an hour later, the ward would have emptied out. The phrase haunted him. Ward khali ho jata. People would have died. Not in a gang war. Not in revenge. In a hospital corridor. For the first time since becoming king, Vardaan understood the scale of responsibility he had chosen. A throne was not only power. It was a burden.

Two days later, another message reached Bharat Furnace. Not through spies. Not through violence. Through a medical volunteer intercepted on the highway. Inside her bag was a folded note. Only one line. "*Yeh Mahamari khatam hoga. War nahi. — Pratap*" Aarohi read the note first.

— He's escalating psychologically now.

Vardaan took the paper silently. Then burned it over an ashtray.

— No, he said quietly.

— He's reminding me what he thinks I've forgotten.

That night, Mahender Suri agreed to one more conversation from Varanasi. His voice sounded weaker than before. Fear had aged him rapidly.

— Aap sahi thein, Vardaan said.

— Bajwa ne ek dusra parallel network banaya hai.

Mahender exhaled slowly.

— Sirf network nahi.

A pause.

— Ek pura Fauj.

Vardaan remained silent. The old man continued:

— Logistics men. Transport captains. Warehouse guards. Local political workers. Ex-policemen. Smugglers. Sab hi apna bafadaari nibha raha hai. Par khulla nahi.

— bhairav ke bhrosa raha to woh kahe ee sab banaye?

Mahender laughed bitterly.

— bharosa hi wah vajah hai jiski vajah se wah ise bana saka.

Then came the sentence that changed everything:

— marne se kuch samay pehle bhairav singh ko sacchai ka kuch hissa pata chala..

The room went still.

— aapko kaise malum?

— kyonki woh khud mere paas aaye the.

Mahender's voice trembled.

— unhone mujhse bajwa se jude sabhi chhipe hue transport record mange, unhone kaha, 'Mahender, koi humare ghar ke neeche surang khod raha hai.

Someone is digging tunnels beneath our house.

— Aaur phir?

Long silence. Then:

— teen hafte bad, vairav ki maut ho gai.

Outside Bharat Furnace, rain began falling over the silent coal belt. Masked workers moved between relief camps carrying sacks of food. Ambulances cut through empty highways. Police barricades glowed under floodlights. India was fighting a pandemic. But inside the Singh Empire, another disease had already spread decades earlier. Ambition. Secrecy. Inheritance. Vardaan looked at the old photograph on his desk: Vairav. Jay Singh Bajwa. Savitri. Vikram. Pratap. Himself. A family before the fire. Then he looked toward the furnace windows, where flames reflected against the night. And for the first time, he understood the shape of the trap. Jay Singh Bajwa had not merely built an empire. He had built a replacement for it.

CHAPTER TWENTY-THREE

THE OXYGEN KING

Coal Belt, May–June, 2020

Death had changed its face. For generations, the Coal Belt knew death. Death came through cave-ins. Through gang wars. Through political assassinations. Through hunger. Through greed. Through coal. But now death has arrived differently. Invisible. Silent. Breathing through the lungs of men.

Every morning brought fresh numbers. More infections. More shortages. More fear. More funerals. And for the first time in decades, people no longer feared gangsters. They feared air.

At Bharat Furnace, Vardaan stood inside the converted control room, staring at a wall-sized map. Red markers covered Bihar. Yellow markers covered Jharkhand. Every marker represented a hospital. Every black marker represented a shortage. Every shortage represented lives.

Ramdeen entered quietly.

— Ranchi se call aail baa.

A call from Ranchi.

Vardaan picked up immediately. The voice on the other side sounded exhausted.

— Sir...

A doctor.

— Humni ke paas teen ghanta oxygen baaki baa. Agar auri marij aihen t uho na tik pai.

We only have three hours of oxygen left. If more patients come that too won't last.

Three hours. Three hours before hundreds began suffocating. The doctor continued.

— Government supply atkal baa."

Government supply is delayed.

— Private supplier loot macha dele baa.

Private suppliers are looting everyone.

Vardaan looked toward the map. Then spoke calmly.

— Hospital ke location bheji.

Send the location.

— Sir?

— Bas location bheji.

Just send the location.

The call ended.

Ramdeen looked at him.

— Pratap ke log route control karat baa.

Pratap's men control those routes.

Vardaan grabbed his jacket.

— Tab route hum khoalb.

Then I'll open the route.

Six trucks. Twenty armed escorts. Forty oxygen cylinders. One objective. Reach Ranchi. No matter what stood in between. The convoy left Bharat Furnace before sunrise. For hours everything remained quiet. Too quiet. The roads looked abandoned. Police barricades. Medical checkpoints. Empty dhabas. Closed petrol pumps. India had become a ghost country. Around noon, they entered a forest stretch outside Hazaribagh. The first truck exploded. The blast shook the entire highway. Trees trembled. Metal flew. Men screamed.

— AMBUSH!

Gunfire erupted immediately. Pratap's men emerged from both sides of the forest. Masks covering their faces. AK rifles in their hands. The pandemic had changed nothing. Only the battlefield. Vardaan stepped out of his SUV. Bullets ripped through nearby vehicles. His commander shouted:

— Malik! Neeche!

Get down!

Vardaan ignored him. Instead he looked toward the oxygen truck. The truck carrying life. And suddenly something inside him snapped. A year ago he would have protected territory. Money. Business. Power. Today he was protecting breath itself. He drew his rifle. Then advanced. The firefight lasted twenty minutes. Twenty brutal minutes. By the end: Nine attackers were dead. Five captured. The convoy survived. And Ranchi received its oxygen. That night every local news channel carried the story. Not about gang warfare. About a businessman, alleged mafia, who personally escorted medical supplies through an armed ambush. The legend grew.

The name spread through WhatsApp groups first. Then newspapers. Then villages. Then labor camps. Workers began saying:

— Vardaan Singh na.

Not Vardaan Singh.

— Oxygen King.

The Oxygen King. A title nobody planned. A title nobody could control. Yet it spread faster than the virus itself. At first Vardaan hated it. Then ignored it. Eventually he accepted it. Because titles rarely belong to the man who receives them. They belong to the people who create them.

While Vardaan fought on roads, Aarohi fought inside archives. The lockdown made everything difficult. Government offices opened only partially. Records disappeared. Files remained inaccessible. Witnesses refused meetings. Yet one clue kept pulling her forward. The cancelled meeting. The final meeting Vairav Singh scheduled before his murder. The question haunted her. *Who was he going to meet? And why did he never arrive?* After weeks of searching, she finally found the answer inside an old district administrative diary. A handwritten appointment note.

Date: Two weeks before Vairav's murder.

Meeting Participants: Vairav Singh, Retired Judge S.K. Sharma, Investigative Officer Rajendra Mishra

Purpose: Confidential.

Aarohi immediately tracked down Rajendra Mishra. Retired. Living near Patna. Seventy-two years old. When she mentioned Vairav's name, the old officer fell silent. For nearly thirty seconds. Then quietly said:

— So he finally sent someone.

Aarohi froze.

— What do you mean?

The old man sighed.

— Vairav knew.

Her heartbeat accelerated.

— Knew what?

Another silence. Then:

— That someone inside the Empire was preparing a coup.

Bharat Furnace, 1999

The wound had become ambition. Jay Singh Bajwa no longer measured success by what he possessed. He measured it by what Vairav possessed. Every achievement became a comparison. Every praise became an insult. Every celebration became a humiliation. One evening he entered Bharat Furnace after a political gathering. The walls were covered with framed photographs. Vairav with ministers. Vairav with labor unions. Vairav with district officers. Vairav with villagers. Vairav. Vairav. Vairav. Nothing else.

Jay stood there alone. Looking. Thinking. Calculating. Then quietly removed one photograph. No reason. No audience. Just a private act. The first symbolic rebellion. The first time he imagined an Empire without Vairav.

Patna, Back in the present

Rajendra Mishra finally revealed what he remembered. Years earlier, Vairav approached him secretly. Not as a businessman. Not as a king. As a worried brother.

— He believed money was disappearing.

— Large amounts.

— Hidden transfers.

— Shell companies.

The exact pattern Aarohi had already discovered.

Mishra continued.

— At first he suspected politicians.

Then:

— He followed the money.

Aarohi leaned forward.

— And?

The old man looked directly into Arohi's camera.

— It led toward Jay Singh Bajwa.

The words hit harder than expected. Because now the timeline became undeniable.

Vairav had begun uncovering the conspiracy. Just before dying. Exactly as Mahender Suri suggested.

The next crisis erupted near Dhanbad. A corrupt supplier diverted oxygen cylinders intended for public hospitals. The black market operation involved local officials. Police protection. Political influence. Ordinarily nobody would touch them. Ordinarily. But these were not ordinary times. Thousands gathered outside the warehouse. Workers. Families. Patients. Doctors. Demanding answers. Demanding justice. Demanding Vardaan. When he arrived, the crowd erupted.

— Malik aa gail!

The boss has arrived!

For a moment he felt uncomfortable. This wasn't respect anymore. This was faith. Dangerous faith. The supplier emerged under police escort. Smug. Protected. Confident.

Until Vardaan spoke.

— Kitna cylinder churaile?

How many cylinders did you steal?

The man smirked.

— Proof baa?

Do you have proof?

The crowd roared. Vardaan simply pointed toward the warehouse. His men opened the doors. Hundreds of stolen cylinders stood inside. Silence. Then rage. The crowd nearly lynched him. Only Vardaan's intervention saved his life. Later that night, every major newspaper carried the same headline. *OXYGEN KING EXPOSES MEDICAL BLACK MARKET*. Pratap saw the article too. And for the first time in months— He looked worried.

Near midnight, Aarohi returned to Bharat Furnace. She found Vardaan alone on the rooftop. Watching smoke rise into the dark sky. For several minutes neither spoke. Then she handed him a file. Everything. The judge. The officer. The cancelled meeting. The investigation. The money trail. Vardaan read every page carefully. When finished, he closed the file. And stared toward the horizon.

— Bauji almost found him.

Aarohi nodded.

— Yes.

Another silence.

Then Vardaan whispered:

— Which means Bajwa knew.

Because conspiracies of that size survive through information. If Vairav discovered the truth— Someone warned Bajwa. Someone inside the Empire. The realization chilled both of them. The betrayal wasn't historical. It was systemic. And perhaps— Still active.

Far away, inside a heavily guarded estate hidden beyond the state border, Jay Singh Bajwa sat before multiple television screens. Every channel carried Vardaan's relief work. Every newspaper praised him. Every village spoke his name.

The old man smiled. Not with pride. With recognition. Because he had seen this before. Years ago. In another man. A man named Vairav Singh. The same popularity. The same devotion. The same love from the people. And the same fatal weakness. Jay slowly switched off the television. Then spoke to the darkness.

— History phir se repeat ho raha hai.

History is repeating itself. Outside, monsoon clouds gathered over the Coal Belt. And somewhere beneath the growing storm, the hidden machinery of betrayal began moving once again.

CHAPTER TWENTY-FOUR

BEFORE THE STORM

Coal Belt, August–September, 2020

After months of silence, the roads began breathing again. First came a few trucks. Then buses. Then trains. Then commerce. Then greed. Then violence. India was reopening. The lockdown had weakened. But the scars remained. Entire businesses had vanished. Thousands remained unemployed. Families carried debts they would spend years repaying. And amid that chaos— the Singh Empire stood stronger than before. Not because it made more money. Because it had survived. People remembered who fed them when nobody else did. People remembered who brought oxygen. People remembered who opened roads.

Everywhere Vardaan traveled, workers folded their hands. Truck drivers saluted. Miners shouted blessings. The title followed him now. Everywhere. *Oxygen King*. At first it embarrassed him. Now it worried him. Because legends often stop listening to reality. The monthly Empire council gathered once again. The room looked very different from six months earlier. No panic. No fear. No uncertainty. Only ambition. Maps covered entire walls. Transport routes. Coal corridors. Border checkpoints. Warehouse locations. Political districts. Ramdeen pointed toward the map.

— Pratap ke territory ab sirf pachis percent bachal baa.

Pratap controls only twenty-five percent of his former territory.

Another commander added:

— Uske teen major transport routes collapse ho chuke hain.

Three major transport routes have collapsed.

— Do logistics hubs hum le chuke hain.

We've already captured two logistics hubs.

The Empire was winning. Decisively. Yet Vardaan remained silent. Because something felt wrong. Too easy. The victories felt real. Yet incomplete. As if somebody was allowing them.

While commanders celebrated victories, Aarohi remained trapped inside a different battlefield. Documents. Records. Financial trails. Ghost companies. Shell accounts. Dead witnesses. The deeper she dug— the larger Jay Singh Bajwa became.

Every investigation eventually reached him. But never directly. Always through layers. Through proxies. Through shadows. Through dead ends. Then finally— she found a crack. A forgotten banking dispute from 2002. Nothing extraordinary. A routine civil case. Except one account number appeared repeatedly. An account linked to: *Bharat Infrastructure Cooperative.* A company that officially did not exist anymore.

Yet money from that account had flowed toward: Pratap's early transport syndicate, several shell contractors, Two political organizations, A logistics company currently operating under Bajwa's influence. For twenty years. The same pipeline. The same hidden artery. Aarohi immediately carried the evidence to Bharat Furnace.

Late that night. Inside Vikram's old office. Aarohi placed multiple files across the desk. Vardaan studied them silently. One document. Then another. Then another. Finally:

— Ee sab connect kaise hota?

How does all this connect?

Aarohi took a deep breath. Then pointed toward the center document.

—This.

A financial ledger.

— Every road leads here.

She connected the names. Mahender Suri. Jay Singh Bajwa. Pratap Chauhan. Shell companies. Transport firms. Political fronts.

One by one. Like assembling a skeleton.

Then finally:

— Pratap was never independent.

Silence.

— He was funded.

More silence.

— Prepared.

And then:

— Owned.

The room became still. Because for the first time— they possessed evidence. Not theory. Not suspicion. Evidence. The first bridge connects Pratap directly to Jay Singh Bajwa.

Three days later—Vardaan moved. Not publicly. Not violently. Strategically. Simultaneous operations began across three states. Warehouses. Transport depots. Fuel yards. Storage facilities. Everything connected to Pratap's remaining network. The objective was simple: Destroy logistics. Destroy movement. Destroy revenue. No movement. No empire. Within forty-eight hours— millions disappeared. Dozens arrested. Supply chains collapsed. Entire territories surrendered without resistance. The news spread rapidly. For the first time in years— Pratap Chauhan looked vulnerable.

Somewhere Near The Jharkhand Border

Night., Rain. Pratap sat alone inside an abandoned inspection bungalow. Maps covered the table. Territories marked red. Then crossed out. Again. And again. And again. Every report looked worse than the previous one. A commander finally spoke.

— Bhai...

No response.

— Hum log ilaka lose karat bani.

We are losing territory.

Still silence. Another commander swallowed nervously.

— Log Vardaan ke taraf jaat baa.

People are shifting toward Vardaan. Pratap slowly lit a cigarette.

Then smiled. A smile that frightened everyone present. Because it wasn't anger. It was understanding. Finally he spoke.

— King kaun baa?

Who is the king?

Nobody answered. Pratap laughed.

— Galat sawaal.

Wrong question.

He leaned back.

— King banawat kaun baa?

Who creates the king?

Silence.

Then:

— Jay Singh Bajwa.

The room froze. Because nobody ever spoke that name aloud. Not here. Not in front of others. Yet Pratap had. Without fear. Without hesitation. As though he already understood something everyone else didn't.

Meanwhile Aarohi received another lead. Retired Judge Sharma. The man scheduled to meet Vairav before his death. The man she had been trying to locate for months. Finally agreed to talk. The interview occurred at a secluded farmhouse outside Patna. The old judge looked frail. Yet his memory remained sharp. When Aarohi showed Vairav's appointment record— his face changed immediately.

— Yes.

— I remember.

— What was the meeting about?

The judge remained silent. For several moments.

Then answered:

— Evidence.

Aarohi's heartbeat accelerated.

— What evidence?

The judge looked directly at her. Then quietly spoke.

— Evidence against Jay Singh Bajwa.

Everything stopped.

For a moment the room seemed to lose air. The judge continued.

— Vairav believed someone inside the Empire was preparing to overthrow him.

— And?

— He wanted legal protection before acting.

Aarohi's voice trembled.

— Did he have proof?

The judge nodded.

— Enough to begin proceedings.

Then came the revelation.

— The file disappeared after his murder.

That night Aarohi couldn't sleep. Because the implications were enormous.

If Vairav truly possessed proof— then someone had stolen it.

Which meant: The conspiracy was real. The conspiracy knew Vairav knew. The conspiracy acted before exposure.

The murder suddenly looked less like betrayal. And more like execution. A planned execution. Ordered long before the trigger was pulled. September rains arrived violently. The coal belt flooded. Roads disappeared beneath the water. Mines slowed again. But Vardaan's Empire remained functional. For the first time in decades— every major coal route. Every major transport corridor. Every major furnace network. Operated under one authority. His authority. The Singh Empire had returned. Stronger. Larger. More centralized than ever. Yet standing atop Bharat Furnace that evening— Vardaan felt no satisfaction. Only unease. Because every answer uncovered another question. Every victory uncovered another enemy. Every dead end eventually pointed toward one name. Jay Singh Bajwa.

Hundreds of kilometers away. Inside a heavily guarded estate. Jay Singh Bajwa stood before a giant map. The same map. The same territories. The same Empire. His advisers looked nervous.

— Pratap weakening.

— Vardaan is growing stronger.

— Coal Belt unified.

The reports continued. Bajwa listened quietly. Then smiled. Not once. Twice. Because nothing he heard surprised him. In fact—everything was happening exactly as expected.

Finally he spoke.

— Abhi kahani shuru hui baa.

The story has only begun.

The men exchanged nervous glances. Bajwa walked toward the window. Rain hammered the glass. Far away. Beyond the storm. Beyond the coal belt. Beyond the war. The next phase waited.

And unlike Pratap— Jay Singh Bajwa had never intended to win through strength. Only patience.

That same night. Inside Bharat Furnace. A courier arrived. No name. No return address. No explanation. Only a sealed envelope. Inside lay a single photograph. Old. Faded. Damaged. Taken nearly twenty-five years earlier. Vairav Singh. Jay Singh Bajwa. Young Vikram. Young Pratap. Standing together. Smiling.

Family. At first glance nothing seemed unusual. Then Vardaan noticed the background. A man standing partially hidden behind a transport truck. Watching. Not participating. Observing. The same face appeared in Mahender's records. The same face appeared in the missing financial files. The same face appeared beside Pratap repeatedly. A ghost. A courier. A messenger between empires. Proof. That somebody had been coordinating both sides for decades. And written behind the photograph— in fading ink— were four words: *"Find The Missing Ledger."* Vardaan stared at the message. Rain pounded the furnace roof. Thunder rolled across the Coal Belt. And somewhere in the darkness— the first chapter of the final war quietly began.

CHAPTER TWENTY-FIVE

OPEN ROADS, OPEN GRAVES

October, 2020

The first truck crossed the state border at 4:17 in the morning. Nobody celebrated. Nobody applauded. Nobody even noticed. Yet for the Singh Empire, it marked the beginning of a new age. For seven months, the highways had belonged to silence. To lockdowns. To checkpoints. To fear. Now the roads were opening again. And roads meant movement. Movement meant money. Money meant power. And power always demanded blood. The morning mist rolled across the Grand Trunk Road like a pale ghost. Stretching from Bengal toward Delhi, the ancient highway had witnessed empires rise and fall for centuries. Kings. Invaders. Merchants. Rebels. Now it was preparing to witness another war. At the highest terrace of Bharat Furnace, Vardaan Singh stood alone. Below him, hundreds of trucks waited inside the compound. Engines running. Headlights glowing. Drivers prepared. Convoys assembled. Security teams deployed. The largest transport operation in Singh Empire history. Ramdeen approached quietly. For several moments neither man spoke. Both watched the sea of vehicles below.

— Ek saal pehle..., Ramdeen said softly.

— Humni ke paas kuchho na rahe.

One year ago we had nothing. Vardaan smiled faintly.

— Ab?

And now?

Ramdeen looked toward the trucks.

— Ab sab kuchh baa.

Now we have everything. Vardaan's expression didn't change. Because he knew better. Nobody ever had everything. Especially kings. Kings merely borrowed power until fate came to collect it.

The convoy began moving. Hundreds of trucks rolling through the gates of Bharat Furnace. Like an army marching toward conquest. And for the first time since Vikram's death— Vardaan felt something unexpected. Not relief. Not satisfaction. Not revenge. Excitement.

That realization disturbed him. But not enough to stop.

Three days later. The first attack came. Near Aurangabad. A convoy carrying industrial equipment vanished. Two drivers disappeared. Communication stopped. GPS trackers went dark. Everyone knew whose work it was. Pratap Chauhan. The old rules had returned. That evening the emergency council gathered inside Bharat Furnace. Maps covered every table. Red markers indicated recent attacks. Blue markers showed Singh-controlled routes. Black markers represented disputed territory.

One commander slammed his fist on the table.

— Pratap phir se road capture kare ke koshish karat baa.

Pratap is trying to capture the highways again.

Another added:

— Teen district mein hamaar trucks rok diye gail baa.

Our trucks have been stopped in three districts. The room erupted with arguments. Vardaan listened silently. Then finally spoke.

— Road ke malik kaun?

Who owns the road? The room became quiet. Nobody answered. Because it wasn't a question. It was a challenge. Vardaan stood.

— Hum kal khud jaai.

Tomorrow I will go personally. Ramdeen immediately objected.

— Malik, ab zarurat na baa.

You don't need to do that anymore. But Vardaan was already walking away. Because somewhere deep inside him, the scientist was disappearing. And something else was growing stronger. The king.

The confrontation happened forty-eight hours later. At a disputed toll corridor near the Bihar border. Dozens of transport contractors gathered there. Many had spent months extorting money from Pratap's men. Others were waiting to see who would ultimately win. Nobody wanted loyalty. Everybody wanted survival.

When Vardaan arrived, the crowd parted automatically. The reaction surprised him. Not fear. Not respect. Something more dangerous. Faith. An elderly transporter stepped forward.

— Malik...

His voice trembled.

— Jab lockdown rahal, tab sab log gayab ho gail.

When the lockdown came, everyone disappeared.

— Bas raur log rahni.

Only your people stayed. Others nodded. Another contractor folded his hands.

— Hum Singh Empire ke saath bani.

I stand with the Singh Empire.

Then another. And another. And another. Within an hour, seven transport unions pledged allegiance. Without threats. Without money. Without force. Vardaan had won something more valuable than territory. Belief. And belief always changed men.

Weeks passed. The offensive expanded. The Singh Empire crossed traditional boundaries. Operations appeared in: Eastern Uttar Pradesh, Northern Jharkhand, Western Bengal, Key logistics hubs across Bihar. The expansion was relentless, disciplined, and methodical. Every successful route increased profits. Every captured corridor weakened Pratap. Every victory strengthened Vardaan's confidence. Too much confidence. One evening, Aarohi watched him studying transport maps. For nearly an hour. Finally she spoke.

— You're enjoying this.

Vardaan didn't look up.

— Enjoying what?

— This.

She gestured toward the maps.

— The expansion.

Silence. Then:

— Maybe.

Aarohi's eyes narrowed.

— You used to talk about satellites.

No response.

— You used to talk about Mars.

Still silence

— You used to talk about changing the future.

Finally Vardaan looked up. The expression in his eyes unsettled her.

Because for a moment—

He looked exactly like Vairav. A king. Not a scientist.

— Future badal raha hoon.

I am changing the future. Aarohi didn't argue. But something about that answer frightened her.

Far away, inside a safehouse near the Jharkhand border, Pratap stared at the latest reports. Lost district. Lost route. Lost warehouse. Lost contractors. Lost influence. The pattern had become impossible to ignore. Every day his empire shrank. Every day Vardaan grew. One commander finally lost patience.

— Hum attack karein?

Should we strike?

Pratap remained silent. Another man added:

— Abhi bhi chance baa.

We still have a chance.

Pratap slowly looked toward the window. Rain tapped softly against the glass. Then he laughed. Not loudly. Not happily. Bitterly. Because he understood something none of them did. This war was no longer between him and Vardaan. The battlefield had changed.

The players had changed. Only the pieces remained unaware. Meanwhile Aarohi's investigation accelerated. The mysterious photograph she received earlier, led her toward a forgotten logistics office near Dhanbad. The building had been abandoned for nearly fifteen years. Dust covered everything. Broken furniture. Rotting records. Collapsed shelves. Most people would have walked away. Aarohi didn't.

Something felt wrong. Or perhaps right. After hours of searching, she discovered a hidden compartment behind an old filing cabinet. Inside rested a metal box. Locked. Weathered. Forgotten. And engraved with a symbol she had already seen multiple times. The symbol of Bharat Infrastructure Cooperative. The same shell organization connected to Jay Singh Bajwa.

The same organization is linked to Vairav's secret investigation. The same organization appears in every major conspiracy. Her hands trembled. Because she suddenly understood. The Missing Ledger might actually exist. And if it did— someone had spent decades ensuring nobody found it.

November arrived. And with it came victory. Another transport syndicate surrendered. Then another. Then another. Soon newspapers began publishing headlines openly.

SINGH EMPIRE DOMINATES EASTERN LOGISTICS

VARDAAN CONSOLIDATES COAL BELT POWER

THE OXYGEN KING BECOMES THE HIGHWAY KING

Titles. More titles. More praise. More admiration.

And slowly— almost invisibly— Vardaan began believing them.

Not completely. Not yet. But enough. Enough for arrogance to take root. Enough for caution to weaken. Enough for Jay Singh Bajwa's plan to progress exactly as intended.

Hundreds of kilometers away. Inside an isolated estate. Jay Singh Bajwa listened to reports. Every report sounded disastrous. Vardaan is growing stronger. Pratap is growing weaker. The Singh Empire expanding. Revenue is increasing. Loyalty rising. Yet the old man appeared calm. Almost amused. One adviser finally gathered courage.

— Sir...

Bajwa looked at him.

— Vardaan jeet raha hai.

Vardaan is winning. The old man smiled. Then slowly poured himself a drink.

— Jeet aur haar...

Victory and defeat...

—...dono samay ke saath badalte hain.

Both change with time. He walked toward a large wall map. His finger moved across highways. Across coal routes. Across warehouses. Across territories. Then finally stopped. At Bharat Furnace. The heart of the Empire. The heart of Vardaan. The heart of everything. His smile widened. Because kings rarely fall during defeat. They fall during triumph.

Outside, winter winds began sweeping across the coal belt. The highways remained busy. The convoys kept moving. The Empire kept expanding. And somewhere beyond the horizon— the road to Holi had already begun.

CHAPTER TWENTY-SIX

The Journalist And The King

November 2020

The winter arrived quietly. Not with snow. Not with storms. But with fog. The Coal Belt disappeared beneath a blanket of white every morning. Roads vanished. Mines vanished. Villages vanished. Even Bharat Furnace—the fortress at the heart of the Singh Empire—often emerged from the mist like a ghost from another age. From the terrace of the old administrative building, Aarohi watched the sunrise. Far below, hundreds of workers had already begun their shifts. Coal trucks moved like giant beasts. Security patrols changed positions. Contractors arrived for meetings. Transport operators waited for approvals. Politicians requested appointments. Police officers sought favors.

The Empire never slept. And now— neither did its king. Aarohi turned toward the opposite terrace. As expected, Vardaan was already there. Standing alone. Looking toward the horizon. For months she had observed this ritual. Every morning. Every single morning. No matter how late he slept. No matter how many meetings awaited him. No matter how many enemies hunted him. He spent the first few minutes of every day staring at the sky. Perhaps some small part of the scientist still survived. The man who once dreamed about stars.

Before the earth dragged him back. Before blood replaced ambition. Before legacy became a curse.

After multiple attacks on journalists investigating political corruption, Bharat Furnace's security council unanimously decided Aarohi could no longer remain alone. Three days later— she moved into Bharat Furnace permanently. The workers celebrated her arrival more than she expected. Many already knew her. Many respected her. Many credited her reporting during the pandemic for exposing black-market operations. By evening, half the workers had started referring to her as:

— Bhabhi ji.

Sister-in-law.

The first time she heard it, she nearly choked on her tea. The second time, she laughed. The third time, she stopped correcting them. Ramdeen found this endlessly amusing.

— Hum ta pahile se bolat rahni.

I had been saying this from the beginning.

Aarohi glared at him.

— Chup rahiye.

Be quiet. The old man laughed loudly. From across the courtyard, Vardaan heard the exchange and simply shook his head. For a brief moment— the fortress felt less like an empire. And more like a family. A dangerous illusion. Their partnership deepened naturally.

Every evening, after Empire business ended, they occupied Vikram's old office. Files covered the desk. Photographs covered the walls. Maps covered entire cabinets. For hours they examined records. Compared witness statements. Studied financial trails. Tracked forgotten names. Searching for one thing. The Missing Ledger. The key to understanding Vairav's murder. And perhaps— everything that followed.

One night, near midnight, Aarohi discovered Vardaan asleep in his chair. The sight startled her. Not because he looked powerful. But because he looked exhausted. The king had disappeared. Leaving behind a tired man carrying the weight of an empire. The files remained open. A half-finished cup of coffee sat beside him. Several maps were spread across the desk. Without realizing it, Aarohi smiled. Because for the first time in years— he looked human. Not a legend. Not a warlord. Not a king. Just Vardaan. The boy she once knew.

The conversation happened a week later. Unexpectedly. They were reviewing old Singh family photographs. Most featured Vairav. Many featured political leaders. Some featured workers. Then Aarohi found one photograph. Young Vikram. Young Vardaan. Standing beside a pond. Fishing rods in hand. Laughing. The image felt strange. Because neither looked powerful. Neither looked dangerous. They simply looked happy. Aarohi handed him the photograph. For several moments he stared at it silently. Then smiled. A genuine smile. Rare now.

— Ee din yaad baa.

I remember this day.

— What happened?

The smile widened.

— He cheated.

Aarohi laughed.

— Vikram cheated?

— Bilkul.

Absolutely.

For the next twenty minutes, Vardaan told stories she had never heard before. Stories about childhood. Stories about school. Stories about festivals. Stories about fights. Stories about brothers. Not kings. Not gangsters. Brothers. The more he spoke, the more alive Vikram became. A protector. A mentor. A troublemaker. A dreamer. The man behind the myth. Eventually silence returned. And then Vardaan quietly said:

— Hum unkar antim din ke baare mein bahut sochat bani.

I think about his last day often.

Aarohi looked at him.

— What about it?

His eyes remained fixed on the photograph.

— Ka soch rahe honge?

What was he thinking?

The question lingered. Because neither had an answer. Only ghosts.

Three days later, Aarohi received a call. The call came from Kolkata. An archivist. A woman she had hired months earlier to investigate old adoption records. At first the conversation seemed routine. Then the archivist said something strange. Very strange.

— Your records don't match.

Aarohi sat upright immediately.

— What do you mean?

The woman hesitated. Then continued.

— The dates are inconsistent.

— How?

— The adoption registration occurred before legal processing.

Silence. Aarohi frowned. That wasn't possible. The archivist continued.

— And several signatures appear altered.

Now her pulse quickened.

— Altered?

— Yes.

Another pause.

— As if someone intentionally changed information.

The room suddenly felt colder. Because journalists developed instincts. And her instincts were screaming. Something was wrong. Very wrong.

Two days later, the archivist sent copies. Dozens of documents. Birth records. Hospital records. Adoption papers. Legal certifications. Municipal registrations. Aarohi spent the entire night reviewing them. At first everything appeared normal. Then patterns emerged. A missing signature. A changed date. A different handwriting style. An erased notation. Individually insignificant. Together, alarming. Near dawn she discovered the most disturbing detail. *"Her original birth certificate had been replaced"*. Not amended. Replaced. The original file no longer existed. Only a duplicate remained. And somebody had worked very hard to make sure nobody noticed. That creates a question on her existence and roots itself.

The next evening she sat alone inside her room. The documents spread across the bed. For years she had investigated powerful men. Corrupt politicians. Business empires. Criminal syndicates. Yet she had never investigated herself. Now she was. And she hated what she found. Because the evidence suggested a terrifying possibility. She didn't know who she really was. The realization frightened her more than any gangster ever had.

Meanwhile, Vardaan faced a different challenge. Success. The most dangerous enemy of all. Every district he entered welcomed him. Every union pledged loyalty. Every contractor sought protection. The Empire continued expanding. And so did his confidence. One afternoon a delegation arrived from Eastern Uttar Pradesh. Transport leaders. Coal traders. Warehouse operators. All requesting Singh protection. After they left, Ramdeen smiled.

— Malik, ee ta Vairav Singh ke samay mein bhi na bhail rahe.

Even during Vairav Singh's era, this never happened.

Vardaan remained quiet. But inwardly— he felt pride. A dangerous pride. Because somewhere deep inside, he had begun believing he was destined for this. Not chosen by circumstance. Destined. Exactly the kind of thinking that destroyed empires.

Three nights later, Aarohi made a breakthrough. One tiny detail. Buried inside an old hospital transfer register. A single handwritten note. No names. No explanations. Only initials. P.C. Beside the record of an infant transfer. The same date associated with her adoption. The same year. The same city. The same timeline. Her hands began trembling. Because she already knew one powerful man whose initials matched. Pratap Chauhan. Immediately she rejected the thought. Impossible. Ridiculous. Coincidental. Yet the possibility refused to disappear. Instead it grew. Like poison. Like fear. Like the truth.

That night she found Vardaan once again standing on the terrace. The winter fog had swallowed the entire Coal Belt. Only the lights of Bharat Furnace remained visible. Like stars trapped on earth. Neither spoke for several minutes. Then Aarohi finally asked:

— Agar kal sab kuchh khatam ho jaye...

Vardaan looked at her.

— Kya?

— Yeh ladai.

She stepped closer.

— Yeh Empire.

Another step.

— Yeh badla.

Another.

— Tab aap kya karenge?

For the first time in months, he didn't answer immediately. Instead he looked upward. Toward the stars hidden behind fog. Toward the sky he once dreamed of conquering. Then he smiled sadly.

— Hum nahi jaane.

I don't know. The answer hurt more than she expected. Because it was honest. The Empire had consumed him. So completely that he could no longer imagine life beyond it.

Far away. Beyond the Coal Belt. Beyond the highways. Beyond the Empire. Jay Singh Bajwa sat alone inside his private study. A file rested on the table before him. A thin file. Old. Worn. Dangerous. Inside it lay secrets buried for decades. Secrets involving Vairav. Pratap. And a little girl. Jay opened the file briefly, looked at a photograph, then closed it again. A faint smile crossed his face. Because some truths were more destructive than bullets. And soon— very soon— those truths would reach the people they were meant to destroy.

Outside, winter deepened. Inside Bharat Furnace, the king and the journalist stood together beneath the fog. Neither realizing that the next revelation would not expose an enemy. It would expose blood itself.

CHAPTER TWENTY-SEVEN

GHOSTS OF BHARAT FURNACE

Bharat Furnace, December, 2020

The dead were speaking again. Not through voices. Not through dreams. But through documents. And documents, Vardaan had learned, were often more dangerous than bullets. A cold wind swept across Bharat Furnace. The massive chimneys stood silent against the winter sky. Once they had carried smoke. Now they carried memories. From the highest balcony of the administrative block, Vardaan watched hundreds of workers begin their shifts. The Singh Empire had survived the lockdown. It had survived the transport war. It had survived Pratap Chauhan. At least for now.

But something had changed. Something invisible. Something he couldn't shoot. Couldn't threaten. Couldn't conquer. The feeling had started after the photograph. The one recovered during the Siege of Bharat Furnace. The photograph that showed three men standing together decades ago. Vairav Singh. Jay Singh Bajwa. And a teenage Pratap. The image had destroyed the official version of history. Because according to every record— Pratap was supposed to have entered the Singh family's life years later.

The photograph proved otherwise. Someone had lied. For decades. And Vardaan intended to find out who. The discovery happened by accident. Like most dangerous discoveries. Two workers repairing water damage beneath the old furnace complex found a sealed iron door hidden behind a collapsed wall. The door shouldn't have existed. According to official blueprints— nothing was supposed to be there. The workers immediately informed security. Within an hour, Bharat Furnace was under lockdown.

By evening, Vardaan, Aarohi, Ramdeen, and the Empire's security chief stood before the rusted entrance. The lock looked ancient. Ramdeen stared at it. Then his face turned pale.

— Ee jagah...

His voice trembled.

— Kaa? Vardaan asked.

The old man swallowed.

— Hum sochni ee kamra kab ke mita diye gail rahe.

I thought this room had been destroyed years ago. Silence. For the first time in months— Vardaan saw genuine fear in Ramdeen's eyes. That frightened him. Because Ramdeen feared almost nothing. The lock was broken. The door slowly opened. A cloud of dust escaped. Decades-old air. Decades-old secrets. Inside stood a forgotten office. Untouched. Undisturbed. Preserved like a tomb. A wooden desk. Steel cabinets. Old maps. Photographs. Files. Ledgers. Newspapers. And on the wall— a framed photograph of Vairav Singh. The room belonged to him. Nobody spoke. Because suddenly Bharat Furnace no longer felt like headquarters. It felt like a graveyard.

The files consumed the next three days. Dozens of boxes. Hundreds of documents. Thousands of pages. Aarohi practically moved into the room. Every record was photographed. Catalogued. Cross-referenced. Analyzed. And slowly— a terrifying picture emerged. Vairav Singh had been conducting a secret investigation before his death. Not against rival gangs. Not against politicians. Against someone inside his own circle. Against Jay Singh Bajwa. The realization stunned everyone. Because history remembered them as brothers. Partners. Founders. Yet these files suggested something entirely different. Vairav had been watching him. Tracking him. Questioning him. Years before his murder.

Aarohi spread several documents across the desk. Financial ledgers. Property transfers. Shell companies. Fake ownership structures. All linked to one name. Jay Singh Bajwa. She looked toward Vardaan.

— aapke bauji ko malum tha..

The room fell silent.

— Kaa malum rahe?

Her answer came quietly.

— ki bajwa chori kar raha tha.

Even Ramdeen looked shocked. Because the evidence was overwhelming. Land diverted. Coal contracts rerouted. Profits hidden. Territories quietly transferred. For years. And Vairav had discovered it. Months before he died.

On the fourth day, Ramdeen finally broke. For years he had hidden certain truths. Out of loyalty. Out of fear. Out of guilt. Now he could no longer remain silent. That evening they sat around an old wooden table inside the secret office. Outside, winter fog swallowed Bharat Furnace. Inside, ghosts waited. Ramdeen stared at Vairav's photograph. Then began speaking.

— Baat bahut purana ba.

This story is very old.

— Humni ke samjhat rahni ki Bajwa babu aur Vairav babu ek jaan rahni.

We thought Bajwa and Vairav were one soul. He smiled sadly.

— Galat rahni.

We were wrong.

The old man described the final years before Vairav's death. The arguments. The disagreements. The growing distance. The jealousy.

And for the first time— he spoke about Savitri. Vardaan's mother. A name rarely mentioned. Almost sacred. Ramdeen hesitated. Then continued.

— Bajwa babu ke nazar bahut pehle se rahal.

Bajwa had been looking at her for a very long time. Silence. Aarohi looked up immediately. Even Vardaan froze. The implication was enormous. Ramdeen lowered his head.

— Vairav babu sab jaanat rahni.

Vairav knew everything.

The room became suffocating. Because suddenly decades of history looked different. Not like politics. Not like business. Like betrayal. Personal betrayal. The most dangerous kind.

Three days later — the witnesses started dying. The first was an accountant. Retired. Seventy-two years old. Living quietly near Dhanbad. Found dead in his home. Official cause: heart attack. The second was a former transport manager. Hit by a truck. The third disappeared entirely. No body. No evidence. No trace. Only silence. Aarohi immediately noticed the pattern. All three names appeared inside Vairav's hidden files. All three possessed information regarding Bajwa. Coincidence was impossible. Someone was cleaning history. Again. Exactly as they had done decades earlier.

The realization reached Vardaan that night. Someone knew what they were investigating. Someone inside the Empire. Because the hidden room had remained secret for decades. Only a handful of people even knew it existed. Yet the witnesses were dying immediately after discovery. Information was leaking. Which meant— the enemy was close. Very close. For the first time since becoming king— Vardaan stopped trusting everyone. Including people he had known for years. Especially people he had known for years. Because betrayal rarely came from strangers. It came from family.

While Vardaan searched for traitors— Aarohi continued investigating her own past. The adoption records. The hospital transfers. The altered signatures. The initials. P.C. She had convinced herself it was a coincidence. Now she wasn't so sure. One evening she received another package. This one from Ranchi. Inside lay an old orphanage register. Mostly damaged. Mostly unreadable. But one page survived. And on that page— a handwritten note. *"Infant transferred under instruction of P.C."* Again. The same initials. The same year. The same timeline. The same mystery. Her hands trembled.

Because every road now pointed toward one man. Pratap Chauhan. The man Vardaan hated more than anyone alive. The man she had spent years investigating. The man connected somehow to her own existence. She closed the file. Immediately. Because she wasn't ready. Not yet.

A week later, Vardaan assembled his inner council. Security chiefs. Regional commanders. Political allies. Business operators. The most powerful people in the Singh Empire. The meeting lasted six hours. At its conclusion, Vardaan delivered a simple order.

— Sabke jaanch hoga.

Everyone will be investigated. Nobody objected. Nobody dared. Yet the room changed instantly. Trust vanished. Suspicion arrived. Exactly as Jay Singh Bajwa would have wanted. And somewhere far away— the old mastermind smiled.

The final shock arrived at midnight. A vehicle approached Bharat Furnace. Alone. Without security. Without escort. The guards almost opened fire. Until they recognized the passenger. An old man. Thin. Injured. Terrified. The moment Ramdeen saw him— he nearly collapsed.

— Arre Bhagwan...

Dear God...

The man had supposedly been dead for fifteen years. Yet here he stood. Breathing. Shaking. Alive. His name was Harbans Lal. Former accountant of the original Singh Empire. One of Vairav's closest confidants. And according to official records— he died long ago. The old man entered Vairav's secret room. Looked at the photograph. Then looked directly at Vardaan. For several moments nobody spoke. Finally— he whispered:

— Humra aane mein bahut der ho gaayil ba.

I have come very late.

Vardaan leaned forward.

— aap kya jaante han?

The old man's eyes filled with fear. Because some memories refuse to die. Even after decades.

— Jay Singh Bajwa...

The room froze. The old man's voice cracked.

— Tohar bauji ke maut bass ek haadsa na rahal.

Your father's death was not an accident.

Silence. Absolute silence. Even the wind outside seemed to stop. Harbans continued.

— Vairav Singh sach ke bahut kareeb pahunch gail rahal.

Vairav Singh had come too close to the truth.

— aur uske liye...

He swallowed.

—...okra marne padhal.

Nobody moved. Nobody breathed. Because for the first time— a living witness had directly connected Jay Singh Bajwa to Vairav's death. Not a rumor. Not a theory. Not a suspicion. A witness. And every person inside the room understood the same thing. If Harbans Lal was telling the truth— then the war was no longer about Vikram. No longer about Pratap. No longer about territory. It was about forty years of lies. And somewhere beyond the winter fog— the architect of those lies was already preparing his next move. Because Jay Singh Bajwa had not survived this long by allowing witnesses to live. And Harbans Lal had just signed his own death warrant.

CHAPTER TWENTY-EIGHT

The Last Loyal Men

January, 2021

The old kingdom was waking up. Not the empire. The kingdom. There was a difference. Empires were built with money. Kingdoms were built with loyalty. And loyalty never truly died. It simply waited. The winter fog had thickened across Bihar and Jharkhand. Coal trains moved like black ghosts through white landscapes. The highways belonged to the Singh Empire once more. The transport unions had surrendered. The coal routes had reopened. The brick kilns were burning again. By every visible measure— Vardaan Singh was winning. Yet inside Bharat Furnace, nobody felt victorious. Because Harbans Lal's testimony had changed everything. For the first time, Jay Singh Bajwa was no longer a shadow. No longer a rumor. No longer a theory. He was becoming real. Vardaan just can not imagine, the man who practically raised him, who was there as his support system, a pillar, when he first returned to India, is the betrayer, the killer of his father. And that terrified everyone. Because Pratap Chauhan was dangerous. But Jay Singh Bajwa was patient. And patient men were always more dangerous.

Three days after Harbans Lal arrived, sealed messages began leaving Bharat Furnace. No emails. No phones. No digital communication. Only handwritten letters. Carried by trusted men. Letters bearing a symbol that had not been used in years. The original seal of Vairav Singh. The message was simple. *"The King calls his brothers home."* Nothing more. Nothing less. The response arrived quickly. Because old loyalties moved faster than modern technology. The first man arrived from Hazaribagh. The second from Gaya. The third from Dhanbad. The fourth from a village nobody had heard of in twenty years. All old. All scarred. All dangerous. All former commanders of Vairav Singh. Men who had built the empire. Men who had fought beside him. Men who had disappeared after his death. Everyone called them bygones. The underworld called them ghosts.

The most feared arrived last. Raghuveer Singh. Not related by blood. But closer to Vairav than most family members. Seventy years old. White beard. Damaged eye. Walking stick. And still capable of terrifying entire rooms. The moment he entered Bharat Furnace, workers stopped what they were doing. Some recognized him. Most knew only the stories. Stories of coal wars. Stories of land battles. Stories from the days before politicians controlled everything. Raghuveer entered the conference hall. Looked at Vardaan. And remained silent. For almost a minute. Then— he slapped him. The room exploded. Security guards rushed forward. Weapons appeared.

— Ruk jaiye!

Vardaan shouted. Everyone froze. Raghuveer stared at him.

— Tani bohot der lagal.

You took too long.

The old man's voice shook with emotion.

— Hum sochni tu kabhi lautbe na.

I thought you would never return.

Then he embraced him. And for the first time since Vikram's funeral— Vardaan felt something he had not felt in years. Family.

The gathering lasted two days. Maps covered the walls. Files covered the tables. Weapons covered the floors. Old commanders met new commanders. Old soldiers met new soldiers. Stories filled the room. And gradually— a forgotten history emerged. One that had never appeared in official records. One that terrified Aarohi.

Because every story pointed toward the same conclusion. Jay Singh Bajwa had been manipulating events for decades. Not openly. Quietly. Patiently. Like a man planting poison beneath a tree. Waiting years for it to die. Harbans Lal spent hours speaking. Describing hidden financial networks. Fake companies. Secret land acquisitions. Political investments. A parallel empire. Built beneath Vairav's empire. Invisible. Until now.

On the third night— the first loyalist died. Commander Yusuf Khan. Former transport chief. Found dead outside a mosque. Three bullets. Professional hit. No witnesses. No evidence. Only a message. Written in blood. *"Some ghosts should remain buried."* The room fell silent when the news arrived. Because everyone understood. Jay Singh Bajwa had responded. The hunt had begun.

That night, Vardaan couldn't sleep. For the first time in months— victory felt distant. Because every answer revealed another question. Every witness revealed another secret. Every clue revealed another lie. He walked alone through Bharat Furnace. Past sleeping workers. Past security checkpoints. Past the giant furnaces. Eventually he reached the hidden room. Vairav's room. His father's room. The desk remained exactly as they had found it. Files. Maps. Photographs. And on the wall— Vairav Singh. Watching. Judging. Waiting. Vardaan stared at the photograph. Then quietly asked:

— Ka sach mein Bajwa hi rahal?

Was it really Bajwa?

The room offered no answer. Only silence.

Meanwhile— Aarohi's own investigation was becoming dangerous. The orphanage records. The hospital transfers. The altered documents. The initials. Everything kept leading back toward Pratap Chauhan. Every road. Every witness. Every forgotten record. And she hated it. Because if the truth was real— everything she believed about herself would collapse. That night she sat alone inside the archive room. Stacks of files surrounded her. One document after another. One clue after another. Then she found something new. A hospital payment receipt. The signature section was partially destroyed. But not completely. The first name remained visible. *Pratap*. Nothing else. Only that. Yet it was enough. Enough to terrify her. Enough to make her hide the document. Because she wasn't ready to tell Vardaan. Not yet.

The old commanders immediately understood the danger. Within days— Bharat Furnace transformed. Watchtowers expanded. Perimeter defenses doubled. Roadblocks appeared. Safe houses activated. The fortress became a fortress again. Exactly as it had been during Vairav's reign. Workers joked that war had returned. The commanders knew better. War had never left. It had simply changed clothes.

The attack came during heavy fog. Just before dawn. Perfect timing. Visibility near zero. Security reduced. Workers asleep. Three vehicles approached the eastern gate. Disguised as medical transport. A tactic increasingly common after COVID. The guards almost allowed them through. Almost. Then Raghuveer noticed something. The vehicles carried medical markings. But no oxygen cylinders, or other medical supplies. His instincts reacted immediately.

— Goli chalao!

Open fire!

The night exploded. Gunfire tore through the fog. The vehicles erupted into chaos. Assassins emerged. Automatic weapons. Grenades. Military training. Not gangsters. Professionals. The battle lasted twelve minutes. Twelve violent minutes. When it ended— eight attackers were dead. Three escaped. One survived. Barely. And before dying— he whispered something. Something that froze everyone present.

— Hum Pratap ke aadmi na bani.

I'm not Pratap's man.

Silence. The dying assassin smiled. Blood spilled from his mouth. Then he spoke one final name. Though inaudible, the lips moved. *"Bajwa."* And died.

The next morning, the war council assembled again. Nobody spoke for several minutes. Because now they possessed confirmation. Not a suspicion. Not a theory. Not a rumor.

Confirmation. Jay Singh Bajwa had directly attacked Bharat Furnace. Meaning the old man was afraid. And powerful men only became afraid when their secrets were close to exposure. Harbans Lal stared at the table. His hands trembled. Then he quietly said:

— Abhi tak tu log jung jeetat rahe.

Until now you were winning a war.

He looked toward Vardaan.

— Ab asli jang shuru bhail ba.

Now the real war has begun.

Nobody argued. Because everyone knew he was right. Pratap Chauhan was merely the sword. The hand holding the sword had finally revealed itself. And that hand belonged to Jay Singh Bajwa.

That evening all surviving commanders gathered inside the central courtyard. Workers filled balconies. Security forces lined the walls. Truck drivers. Coal laborers. Brick workers. Contractors. Union leaders. Thousands watched. The old commanders stood beside Vardaan. The final generation of Vairav Singh's loyalists. A dying breed. Yet still standing. Raghuveer stepped forward. Raised his hand. And spoke loudly.

— Jab Vairav Singh giral rahal...

When Vairav Singh fell..

—...tab hum haar gail rahni."

...we were defeated.

His voice echoed across Bharat Furnace.

—Lekin aaj...

But today... He pointed toward Vardaan.

—...Singh Raj phir se khada ba.

...the Singh Kingdom stands again.

Thousands erupted. The roar shook the fortress. Yet Vardaan remained silent. Because for the first time— he understood what he truly possessed. Not territory. Not wealth. Not power. Legacy. And legacy was both a weapon and a curse.

Far away— inside a luxurious estate hidden from public view— Jay Singh Bajwa watched footage from the failed attack. Expressionless. One by one, he studied the faces gathered around

Vardaan. Then his gaze settled on Harbans Lal. The old witness. The man who should have died years ago. A faint smile appeared. Not anger. Not frustration. Calculation. Because Jay Singh Bajwa had spent forty years destroying families. And he knew exactly where to strike next. Not at the king. At the people the king loved.

CHAPTER TWENTY-NINE

MEERA

February, 2021

There were many kinds of power. Power that came from guns. Power that came from money. Power that came from fear. Vardaan Singh possessed all three. Yet there was one kind of power he had never understood. The power to heal, to love. And that power arrived at Bharat Furnace in the form of a woman named Meera.

India was still struggling to recover. The first wave of COVID had weakened. Markets had reopened. Factories had resumed operations. Highways once again carried cargo across the nation. But the scars remained. Every village had lost someone. Every town had buried someone. Every family carried grief. The Singh Empire was no different. Coal miners had died. Truck drivers had died. Brick workers had died. Contractors had died. Entire families who depended on Bharat Furnace had been devastated. For the first time in years, the empire faced an enemy that couldn't be shot. And Vardaan hated that. Because bullets solved nothing. Fear solved nothing. Violence solved nothing. Disease didn't care who ruled. Disease didn't recognize kings.

The idea came from Aarohi.

— You have money.

She said.

—You have manpower.

—You have land.

— Then stop building fortresses for a few weeks and build a hospital.

Vardaan looked at her.

— Hospital?

— Haan.

She folded her arms.

— Log mar rahe hain.

People are dying.

— King banna hai toh pehle logon ko bachao.

If you want to be a king, save your people first. The words stayed with him. For days. And eventually— he agreed. Within a month, a massive temporary medical facility emerged near Bharat Furnace. Oxygen beds. Isolation wards. Emergency units. Medical supplies. Hundreds of workers volunteered. Doctors arrived from Ranchi. Patna. Dhanbad. Kolkata. And among them was Meera Sharma.

The first time Vardaan saw her— she was yelling at a minister. Not politely. Not diplomatically. Simply yelling. The minister had arrived for publicity. Cameras. Media. Security. The usual circus. He wanted photographs. Not patients. Meera stood directly in front of him.

— Sir, oxygen cylinders kahaan hain?

Where are the oxygen cylinders?

The minister smiled.

— Arrangements ho jayenge.

Arrangements will be made.

Meera pointed toward the ward.

— Nahi sir, Abhi, log mar rahe hai.

"People are dying now."

The minister's smile disappeared. Security moved forward. Meera didn't move.

— Photo baad mein khichwaiyega.

Take photographs later.

— Pehle insaano ko bacha lijiye.

Save these human beings first.

The minister left in humiliation. The staff applauded. Meera ignored them. And returned to work. From across the compound— Vardaan watched everything. For the first time in years— he smiled.

A week later— he met her properly. She was treating injured miners. One worker recognized Vardaan. Immediately stood up. Others followed. Within seconds everyone was standing. Almost worshipping. Meera looked confused. Then annoyed.

— Why are they standing?

Nobody answered.

Finally one nurse whispered.

— Vardaan Singh.

Meera turned.

Looked at him. Looked again. Then shrugged.

— Accha.

And continued working. Vardaan blinked. Nobody reacted that way to him anymore. Everyone feared him. Respected him. Obeyed him. This woman barely acknowledged him.

— You know who I am?

he asked.

Without looking up she replied—

— Patient toh nahi hain.

You're not a patient.

— So not important right now.

Several nurses nearly fainted. Vardaan laughed. Actually laughed. A sound nobody around him had heard in months.

The following weeks changed something inside him. He began visiting the hospital regularly. Officially— to inspect operations. Unofficially— to see Meera. At first she ignored him. Then tolerated him. Then occasionally spoke to him. And slowly— something strange happened. She treated him like a human being. Not a king. Not a gangster. Not a legend. A man. One evening she found him sitting outside one ward. Watching patients through the glass. Silent.

— What are you thinking?

she asked. Vardaan remained quiet. For a long moment. Then said—

— In space...

She looked surprised. He continued.

— When you look at Earth from orbit...

—...all borders disappear.

— Countries disappear.

— Religions disappear.

— Power disappears.

— Everything becomes small.

Meera sat beside him. Confused about what he is saying, but listening. For the first time— not to the king. But to the scientist, the man he buried beneath blood and coal, long ago. And Meera didn't know anything about it.

Aarohi noticed immediately. Of course she did. She always noticed everything. One evening she found Meera leaving the hospital.

— Doctor sahiba.

Meera smiled.

— Journalist madam.

The two women began walking together. A silence followed. Then Aarohi spoke.

— Do you know who he was before all this?

Meera looked toward Bharat Furnace. Toward the giant chimneys. Toward the kingdom.

— No.

Aarohi smiled sadly.

— Neither does he.

The answer confused Meera. But she understood something important. Vardaan carried wounds nobody could see. And they were far deeper than bullets.

Weeks passed. The hospital became successful. Thousands received treatment. Hundreds survived. Entire villages praised Bharat Furnace. For the first time— newspapers wrote positive stories about Vardaan Singh. Not gang wars. Not coal routes. Not violence. Healthcare. Relief work. Food distribution. Meera became the face of the effort. Workers adored her. Women trusted her. Children followed her everywhere. And slowly— Bharat Furnace began feeling alive again. Like a home. Not a fortress. One evening a small girl approached Vardaan. Perhaps eight years old.

— Dada.

He looked down. She handed him a drawing. It showed three figures. A furnace. A doctor. And a king. The king was smiling. The doctor was holding his hand. The child pointed.

— E doctor didi ke saath rehna.

Stay with doctor sister.

— Tab aap kam daraawna lagte hain.

Then you look less scary.

The workers burst into laughter. Even Vardaan laughed. But later that night— he kept staring at the drawing. Because the child was right.

A few days later— Vardaan and Meera sat atop Bharat Furnace's highest observation tower. Night covered the coal belt. Thousands of lights glowed below. The empire. His empire. For a long time neither spoke. Then Meera asked—

— Do you ever regret it?

He knew what she meant. Everything. The violence. The war. The blood.

Vardaan stared into the darkness.

— Every day.

Meera looked surprised. Because the answer came immediately. Without hesitation. Without excuses. He continued.

—But if I stop...

—...my people die.

— If I become weak...

—...my people die.

— If I lose...

—...my people die.

His voice became quieter.

—So I keep going.

Meera watched him carefully. Then softly replied—

— Sometimes surviving isn't living.

The words struck him harder than any bullet. Because deep down— he knew she was right.

Days later— Meera found an old storage room. Inside were boxes from America. Research papers. Scientific journals. Engineering notebooks. The life Vardaan had abandoned. She spent hours reading them. Hours understanding who he once was. And that night— she confronted him.

— Why did you stop?

He looked confused.

— Stop what?

She placed the notebooks on the table.

— This.

— Your dream.

Silence. For several moments. Then Vardaan laughed bitterly.

— My brother died.

— My family collapsed.

— My empire burned.

— Dreams don't survive things like that.

Meera stepped closer.

— Maybe they should.

He couldn't answer. Because nobody had ever suggested such a thing before. Everyone wanted the king. Only she seemed interested in the man.

By February 2021— the empire stood stronger than ever. Territories reclaimed. Routes secured. Enemies retreating. The workers celebrated. The commanders relaxed. Even Aarohi allowed herself brief moments of happiness. And that was exactly why it was dangerous. Because wars became deadliest when people believed they were ending. One evening Harbans Lal approached Vardaan. The old man seemed troubled.

— Nazar rakhi.

Keep watching.

Vardaan frowned.

— Kis par?

On whom?

Harbans looked toward the horizon. Toward the darkness beyond the coal belt.

— Sab par.

On everyone.

Then he added quietly—

— Jay Singh Bajwa kabhi jaldi nahi karta.

Jay Singh Bajwa never acts in haste.

— Woh intezaar karta hai.

He waits.

— Jab log khush ho jaate hain.

Until people become happy. The words lingered long after the old man left. Because deep inside— Vardaan felt something he hadn't felt in years. Hope. And hope was often the first victim of war.

Hundreds of kilometers away— Jay Singh Bajwa received a report. He read silently. No emotion. No reaction. Only observation. Then he reached for a photograph. Meera. Standing beside Vardaan. Laughing. The old man's eyes narrowed. A dangerous smile appeared. Then quietly said—

— Ab samjha.

Now I understand.

Because after decades of war— he recognized a pattern. Every Singh man eventually found something worth living for. And that made them vulnerable. Vairav had Savitri. Vikram had Nandini. Now Vardaan had Meera. Jay Singh Bajwa folded the photograph. Carefully. Then placed it inside a file. A file labeled: LEVERAGE

The old man's smile returned. Cold. Patient. Merciless. Because after years of destroying dynasties— he had finally discovered Vardaan Singh's weakness. And unlike Pratap— Jay Singh Bajwa never missed twice.

CHAPTER THIRTY

THE FALSE VICTORY

March, 2021

The first time Vardaan Singh met Pratap Chauhan, he wanted to kill him. The second time— he wanted answers. That frightened him more. Because hatred was simple. Questions were dangerous. For nearly two years, the war had consumed eastern India. Coal routes. Transport corridors. Political influence. Land contracts. Brick industries. Entire districts. Thousands had chosen sides. Hundreds had died. Millions of rupees had burned. And yet— the one question that had started everything remained unanswered. Why did Pratap kill Vikram? Not how. Not when. Not where. "*Why*". That question haunted Vardaan more than any battlefield. Because every new discovery seemed to contradict the old story. Harbans Lal's testimony. The photograph of Vairav. The teenage Pratap. Jay Singh Bajwa standing beside them. The missing records. The dead witnesses. Nothing made sense. And when nothing made sense— Vardaan trusted only one thing. Face-to-face conversations. The meeting was arranged through intermediaries. Old channels. Old loyalties. Old rules. A neutral ground. No armies. No snipers. No hidden weapons. No ambushes. A place sacred enough that even gangsters respected it. The abandoned railway repair yard outside Dhanbad. A forgotten relic of another era. Rusting locomotives. Broken tracks. Collapsed workshops. A graveyard of industry. Perfect for two dying kings.

Vardaan arrived first. Only one vehicle. Only one driver. No convoy. No bodyguards. Against every security recommendation. Raghuveer had nearly exploded when he heard.

— Pagal ho gail baa?

Have you lost your mind?

— Ohi aadmi se milat baa je Vikram ke maar delas?

You're meeting the man who murdered Vikram?

But Vardaan had already decided. Because some answers could not be delegated. Some ghosts had to be faced personally. The winter sun was fading when another vehicle appeared. Black SUV. No escort. No protection. Just one man. Pratap Chauhan. For a moment neither moved. Years of hatred stood twenty feet apart. The murderer. The brother. Both kings. Both exhausted. Both carrying too many dead men on their shoulders. Finally Pratap spoke.

— Bahut der laga dihal.

Took you long enough.

Vardaan didn't smile.

— Tohar maut ke intezaar karat rahni.

I was waiting for your death.

Pratap laughed. A tired laugh. The laugh of a man who had heard worse.

They sat inside an abandoned workshop. Dust covered everything. Broken machinery surrounded them. Sunlight filtered through shattered windows. No cameras. No witnesses. Only history. For several minutes neither spoke. Then Vardaan finally asked:

— Kahe?

Why?

Pratap knew what he meant. Everyone knew. Why Vikram? The older man stared toward the broken railway tracks. For a long time. Then quietly said:

— Galat Sawal.

Wrong question. Vardaan's jaw tightened. Pratap continued.

— Sawal ee na ba ki hum Vikram ke kahe maarni.

The question isn't why I killed Vikram.

— Sawal ee ba ki hum uss din tak pahunchal kaise.

The question is how I became the man who could kill him.

Silence. The answer unsettled Vardaan immediately. Because it didn't sound like an excuse. It sounded like regret.

For the first time— Pratap spoke about Vikram. Not as an enemy. Not as a victim. As a brother.

— Tohar bhai...

Your brother...

The words caught in his throat.

—...bahut bada aadmi rahal.

...was a great man.

Vardaan stared. Confused. Because hatred had prepared him for many things. Not admiration. Pratap smiled faintly.

— Hum bhookha rahni.

I was hungry.

— Anath rahni.

I was an orphan.

— Koi naam na rahal.

I had no name.

Then he looked directly into Vardaan's eyes.

— Naam Vikram Singh dihalas.

Vikram Singh gave me one.

The room fell silent. Because suddenly— the photograph from Bharat Furnace felt real. The teenage boy. The young Vikram. The forgotten past. Not mythology. Reality.

For the first time— certainty cracked. Not Pratap's certainty. Vardaan's. Because if Vikram had truly loved Pratap— then why had everything ended in murder? The contradiction was impossible. And yet— the pain in Pratap's eyes was real. Not performed. Not manipulated. Real.

Eventually Vardaan asked the question that had been growing inside him for months.

—Jay Singh Bajwa.

Pratap froze. Only for a second. But Vardaan saw it. Saw the reaction. Saw the fear. Because it wasn't anger. It wasn't hatred. Fear. And that terrified Vardaan more than anything. Because Pratap Chauhan feared almost nobody. Yet he feared that name. The older man slowly stood. Walked toward a broken locomotive. Touched the rusted steel. Then spoke quietly.

— Tohar baba ke sab log jaanat rahe.

Everyone knew your father.

— Vikram ke sab jaanat rahe.

Everyone knew Vikram.

He turned.

— Lekin asli kahani kabhu na sunal.

But nobody heard the real story.

Vardaan's pulse quickened. For a moment— he thought the truth was finally coming. But Pratap shook his head.

— Abhi na.

Not yet.

The meeting was ending. Both men knew it. Outside— darkness had begun swallowing the yard. The war waited. The bloodshed waited. The future waited. Before leaving— Pratap stopped beside the door. For the first time all day— he looked genuinely troubled. Almost concerned. For Vardaan.

— Ek salah de sakat bani?

Can I give you advice?

Vardaan laughed coldly.

— Murderer se?

From a murderer?

Pratap ignored the insult. Then quietly said:

— Je log ke tu sabse jyada pyaar karela...

The people you love most...

—...unke bachake rakha.

Protect them.

Silence. A strange chill moved through the room. Because Pratap wasn't threatening him. He was warning him.

— Ka matlab?

What does that mean?

Pratap's eyes darkened. For a moment— he looked like a man staring at his own grave. Then he spoke.

— Jang humse na ba.

This war isn't with me. And left.

Neither man noticed the observer. Far beyond the railway yard. Hidden inside a water tower. A man with a camera. A professional. Not Pratap's. Not Vardaan's. Jay Singh Bajwa's. The photographs were transmitted before midnight. By dawn— they sat on Bajwa's desk. The old man studied them carefully. Vardaan. Pratap. Together. Talking. Learning. Getting closer to the truth. A dangerous development. Very dangerous. Because if those two men ever fully understood the past— everything would collapse. Everything. For several minutes Jay Singh Bajwa remained silent.

Outside Bharat Furnace— spring was slowly approaching. Workers celebrated. Business expanded. Coal moved. Highways prospered. For the first time in years— hope existed. And somewhere deep inside himself— Vardaan allowed himself to believe that maybe the war was nearing its end. He was wrong. The war was only entering its final act. And the first victim of that act had already been chosen. Meera Sharma.

CHAPTER THIRTY-ONE

The Betrayer's Story

Bharat Furnace, Mid April, 2021

The most dangerous thing in war was not an enemy. It was the truth. Because enemies could be killed. Truths survived. The Singh Empire stood stronger than it had in years. Coal routes had reopened. Transport networks stretched across Bihar and Jharkhand. Brick kilns burned day and night. Money flowed. Power expanded. Fear returned.

People once again whispered the old sentence.

— Singh Raj wapas aa gail ba.

The Singh Kingdom has returned.

And at the center of it all stood Vardaan Singh. Not as a scientist. Not as a grieving younger brother. As a king. A king whose name now traveled faster than freight trains. But every empire carried cracks. And Vardaan's crack was invisible. Because it was not inside his business. Not inside his army. Not inside his politics. It was inside his heart.

The old furnace complex had transformed. What was once a dying industrial ruin had become a fortified capital. Control rooms. Transport command centers. Coal logistics hubs. Private security barracks. Political offices. Everything now flowed through Bharat Furnace. Workers had even begun hanging portraits. Vairav Singh. Vikram Singh. Vardaan Singh. Three generations. Three kings. One empire. Meera hated it.

— Yeh sab hataiye.

Remove these. Workers looked confused.

— Kaahe didi?

Why, sister?

She pointed toward Vardaan's portrait.

— Insaan ko bhagwan banaoge toh ek din woh khud ko bhagwan samajhne lagega.

If you make a man into a god, one day he'll begin believing it.

The workers laughed. But Vardaan didn't. Because somewhere deep inside— he knew she was right. And that frightened him.

Three nights later— a package arrived. No sender. No return address. No fingerprints. Only one photograph. Vardaan stared at it. For a very long time. Young Vikram. Young Pratap. Standing together. Arms around each other. Smiling. Brothers. Real brothers. Not enemies. On the back was a sentence. Written in old blue ink. *"Humra se puchha nahi kabhu ki kahani ka ba."* You never asked me what the story really is. No signature. None was needed. Pratap. For the first time— Vardaan felt anger leaving him. And confusion replacing it. Because murderers didn't send memories. They sent threats.

At the same time— Aarohi's investigation reached its final wall. The adoption records. The hospital records. The old police files. Everything led to dead ends. Destroyed documents. Missing pages. Corrupt officials. The pattern itself was suspicious. Someone powerful had erased her history. Deliberately. Finally an elderly retired registrar agreed to meet her. A forgotten government employee. Nearly ninety years old. Almost blind. The meeting took place in a village near Deoghar. The old man listened quietly. Then asked:

—Tohar janam ke saal?

Your birth year?

Aarohi answered. The old man's face changed. Immediately. Recognition. Fear. Memory.

— Na...

No...

He whispered.

— Ee file phir se khul gayil?

That file has opened again?

Aarohi leaned forward.

— Kaa matlab?

What do you mean?

The old man slowly stood, walked to a wooden cupboard, removed a rusted metal box. Inside lay documents older than Aarohi herself. Yellow, fragile, forgotten.

One file carried a single name. *Pratap Chauhan.* Aarohi froze. The old man looked directly into her eyes. Then quietly said:

— Beta...

Child...

— Tohar zindagi jhoot par banal ba.

Your life was built on a lie.

The world stopped. For several seconds. Nobody spoke. Nobody moved. Then he handed her the file. And Aarohi saw the truth. The biological father's section. *PRATAP CHAUHAN.* Her hands began trembling. Again. And again. And again. Until she could barely breathe. Because suddenly— everything changed. The man she had spent years investigating. The man Vardaan wanted dead. The man responsible for Vikram's murder. Was her father.

Elsewhere— hundreds of kilometers away— Jay Singh Bajwa was losing patience. The old general sat alone inside his estate. Reports covered his desk. Failed operations. Lost territories. Dead commanders. Broken alliances. Pratap was weakening. That was expected. But Vardaan wasn't following the script. That was dangerous. Very dangerous. Because Vardaan was supposed to become another Vikram. Predictable. Emotional. Controllable. Instead— he had become something else. A strategist. A survivor. A king. And kings were difficult to manipulate. Unless you attacked what they loved. Bajwa already knew the target. Now he began planning the method.

For decades— Jay Singh Bajwa had built insurance. Not armies. Not politicians. Assets. Invisible assets. Contractors. Police officers. Accountants. Drivers. Doctors. Men nobody noticed. Men who never appeared in photographs. Men who never carried guns. Men who waited. Some had waited twenty years. Some thirty. Now— one by one— their phones began ringing.

A single sentence.

— Samay aa gail ba.

The time has come.

Across Bihar. Across Jharkhand. Across Bengal. Across Uttar Pradesh. The network awakened. And nobody knew. Not Vardaan. Not Pratap. Not Aarohi. Nobody.

Meanwhile— Pratap himself was changing. For years he had believed one thing. That he was fighting for justice. That Vikram deserved punishment. That Vairav had betrayed people. That Bajwa spoke truth. But the cracks had begun appearing. Too many lies. Too many deaths. Too many missing pieces.

And now— even his own commanders were disappearing. Not killed by Vardaan. Vanishing. Silenced. Erased. The same way witnesses had vanished. The same way records had vanished. The same way history had vanished. Pratap finally understood. He wasn't a partner. He was evidence. Evidence that would eventually need destruction. For the first time in decades— Pratap Chauhan became afraid. Not of Vardaan. Of Jay Singh Bajwa.

That night— Aarohi returned to Bharat Furnace. Silent. Broken. The file remained hidden inside her bag. She couldn't tell Vardaan. Not now. Not when the empire stood on the edge of victory. Not when war was reaching its end. Not when Vardaan's entire life revolved around avenging Vikram. Because one revelation could destroy everything. She found Vardaan standing atop the furnace tower. Looking over the empire. Coal lights flickered across the horizon. Thousands of workers. Thousands of families. Thousands of dreams. He smiled when he saw her. A rare smile. The smile of the man she had once loved. Not the king. Not the gangster. The man.

— Kaa bhail?

What happened?

She almost told him. Almost. But the words refused to come. Instead she stepped closer. And hugged him. For a long time. Longer than usual. Because somewhere deep inside— she suddenly felt she was losing him. Not physically. Fatefully. Like history had already chosen a path. And none of them could escape it. Above them— the furnace burned. Below them— the empire expanded.

Far away— Jay Singh Bajwa's network awakened. And somewhere in the darkness— Pratap Chauhan prepared to tell the truth he should have told years ago. The truth that would destroy every certainty. The truth that would turn enemies into victims. Victims into traitors. And traitors into ghosts. Because the story of Vikram Singh's murder had never been about murder. It had always been about betrayal. And betrayal was finally coming home.

CHAPTER THIRTY-TWO

THE HUNTER'S TRAP

July, 2021

Every empire dies twice. First in reality. Then in memory. Pratap Chauhan's empire was now dying in reality. The memory would take longer. For nearly fifteen years, his shadow had stretched across Bihar, Jharkhand and the eastern freight corridors of India. Coal. Transport. Land. Arms. Politics. Fear. Entire districts had whispered his name before sleeping. Now those same districts whispered another. Vardaan Singh. The Red King. The man who had returned from America to reclaim a kingdom everyone believed dead. And he was winning. The operation began before sunrise. Simultaneous strikes. Seven districts. Three highways. Two railway corridors. Four coal depots. Months of planning. Weeks of surveillance. Hours of execution.

Inside Bharat Furnace, maps covered an entire wall. Red markers. Blue markers. Moving pieces. Changing territories. It looked less like a gang war. More like a military campaign. Raghuveer pointed at the eastern sector.

— Deoghar abhi clear ba.

Another commander spoke.

— Giridih surrender kar dihal.

A third added:

— Dhanbad route bhi kabja hui gilan.

Vardaan remained silent. Watching. Calculating. No excitement. No celebration. Because this was no longer revenge. This was a conquest. And conquest demanded discipline. By noon— three of Pratap's largest transport operators had switched allegiance. By evening— two coal syndicates surrendered without a fight. By midnight— an entire logistics network changed hands. The Singh Empire had gained more territory in one day than it had gained in the previous six months. And everyone knew what it meant. Pratap Chauhan was losing.

Three days later— Vardaan entered one of Pratap's abandoned strongholds. A sprawling estate outside Hazaribagh. Once feared. Now empty. The walls carried bullet scars. Broken furniture. Abandoned weapons. Evidence of a retreat. But something else caught Vardaan's attention. Photographs. Dozens. Old. Dust-covered. Forgotten. Many showed Pratap as a young man. Others showed local leaders. Workers. Contractors. Political figures. Then Vardaan found one that froze him. Young Vikram. Young Pratap. Standing beside each other. Smiling. Again. Always together. Brothers. Not enemies. The contradiction became impossible to ignore.

At the same time— Aarohi carried a secret that felt heavier than death. Pratap Chauhan. Her father. The words refused to become real. Every time she repeated them inside her head— they sounded absurd. Impossible. Yet the documents existed. The signatures existed. The dates existed. Truth existed. And truth was merciless. For days she avoided Vardaan. Not because she feared him. Because she feared what would happen if she told him. Would he see her differently? Would he see Pratap every time he looked at her? Would Vikram's ghost stand between them forever? She didn't know. And that uncertainty was killing her.

The last meeting happened at night. Not arranged by intermediaries. Not negotiated. Not planned. Pratap requested it himself. A single message.

— Ab kahani sune ke samay aa gail ba.

It's time to hear the story. The location: An abandoned coal loading station. Half destroyed. Half forgotten. Exactly the kind of place where old ghosts liked to speak. Vardaan arrived alone. Pratap was already there. Sitting atop a rusted conveyor belt. For a long time— neither spoke. Then Pratap finally said:

— Tohar bhai humra se nafrat kabhu na karat rahal.

Your brother never hated me. The sentence hit harder than a bullet. Because Vardaan suddenly realized— Pratap wasn't defending himself. He was mourning.

For the next hour— Pratap spoke. Not as a gangster. Not as a rival. As a younger brother remembering an elder one. He spoke of hunger. Poverty. Street fights. Small victories. How Vikram had protected him. Fed him. Trusted him. How the Singh household became the first place that ever felt like home. And slowly— the image of the monster began cracking. Because monsters did not remember with tears. They remembered with pride. Pratap remembered with pain.

— Hum Vikram bhai ke liye apna jaan de sakat rahni.

I could have given my life for Vikram.

His voice broke.

— Uuka jaan le na.

Not take it. Silence filled the station. Because suddenly— everything felt wrong. The story. The history. The murder. All wrong.

Finally Vardaan asked:

— Phir maaral kaise?

Then how did you kill him?

Pratap closed his eyes. For a very long time. When he finally answered— his voice carried decades of regret.

— Jhoot.

Lies.

— Barso tak jhoot.

Years of lies.

He looked toward the darkness.

— Humra dikhawal gail ki humra saath dhokha bhail.

I was made to believe I had been betrayed.

— Humra dikhawal gail ki Singh parivar humke istemal kailas.

I was made to believe the Singh family had used me.

— Humra dikhawal gail ki Vikram sab jaant rahal.

I was made to believe Vikram knew everything.

Every sentence landed like a hammer. Because Vardaan already knew whose method this sounded like. Manipulation. Isolation. Half-truths. Jay Singh Bajwa.

Pratap reached into his coat. Slowly. Carefully. Then removed a sealed packet. Old papers. Photographs. Letters. Evidence. The kind that killed powerful men. He handed them to Vardaan.

— Ee sab bachake rakha.

Protect these.

— Humse jyada der tak tu bachi.

You will survive longer than me.

The statement stunned Vardaan. Because it sounded like a farewell. Not a warning. A farewell.

Far away— inside a fortified estate— Jay Singh Bajwa received terrible news. The offensive had succeeded. Pratap was collapsing. Worse— Pratap had met Vardaan again. Again. The old man immediately understood the danger. Not military danger. Historical danger. Truth. Because if Pratap spoke completely— forty years of lies would begin unraveling. That could not be allowed. Not now. Not ever. For the first time in years— Jay Singh Bajwa abandoned patience.

And activated Phase Two. The phase nobody knew existed. Not Pratap. Not Vardaan. Not Aarohi. Nobody.

When the meeting finally ended— Pratap remained seated. Watching Vardaan walk away. Watching history move toward its destination. The younger man stopped once. Turned. For the first time since Vikram's death— he asked a question without hatred.

— Kaash...

He paused.

—...ee sab pahile batwale rahit.

I wish you had told me all this earlier.

Pratap smiled sadly.

— Hum bhi.

Me too.

The answer carried twenty years of regret. Twenty years that could never be repaired. Vardaan left. Pratap remained behind. Alone. The old coal station groaned beneath the wind. Somewhere in the darkness— unseen eyes watched. Because Jay Singh Bajwa's network had already moved. And for the first time— Pratap Chauhan understood something terrifying. He had survived Vardaan. He had survived gang wars. He had survived politicians. But he might not survive the man who created him. Above the station— storm clouds gathered. And none of them yet understood— that the final moves of the game had already begun. The king. The betrayer. The daughter. The lover. The architect. All moving toward the same destination. Blood.

CHAPTER THIRTY-THREE

THE WEDDING

December, 2021

The winter fog arrived early that year. Every morning, Bharat Furnace disappeared beneath a blanket of white mist before slowly emerging again with the sunrise, as if the old empire was being reborn from its own ashes. For nearly three years, the furnace had witnessed nothing but funerals, betrayals, power struggles, and grief. Now, for the first time, it was preparing for a wedding. And that alone felt miraculous. The Singh Empire stood stronger than it had since Vikram Singh's death. The coal routes were functioning. The transport network had stabilized. Contractors had returned. Factories were operating again after the long disruption of the pandemic years. For ordinary people across the region, the uncertainty of lockdowns and economic collapse was finally beginning to ease. Life was returning. And with life came celebration.

Workers decorated the massive furnace complex with thousands of lights. Old brick kilns became ceremonial gateways. Coal yards were transformed into gathering grounds. Entire villages volunteered to help. Nobody was forced. Nobody was paid. People simply wanted to participate. Because this wasn't merely Vardaan Singh's wedding. To many people, it symbolized survival. An elderly miner stood watching the preparations. His grandson tugged at his hand.

— Dadaji, ee sab ka ho raha ba?

Grandfather, what's happening?

The old man smiled.

— Umeed Khil rahi hai.

Hope is getting back.

Across the complex, drums echoed through the evening. Traditional Bhojpuri wedding songs mixed with modern music. Children ran through the decorated pathways. Women prepared food for thousands of guests. For a brief moment, Bharat Furnace looked less like the headquarters of an empire and more like a home. Yet even in moments of joy, shadows remained. Because every person present carried memories. The memory of Vairav Singh. The memory of Vikram Singh. The memory of years stolen by revenge. Especially Vardaan. He stood alone on a balcony overlooking the celebrations. The winter wind carried distant music through the night. Below him stretched everything he had rebuilt. The empire. The workers. The roads. The factories. The people. But the victory felt strangely incomplete. Because every achievement carried a cost. Every success reminded him of someone who was no longer there to witness it.

— Again thinking too much?

A voice interrupted.

Meera. She stepped beside him carrying two cups of tea. Unlike everyone else, she never approached him like a king. Never treated him like someone feared. Never behaved as if he ruled half the region. She simply treated him like a man. And perhaps that was why he loved her. Vardaan accepted the tea.

— You know me too well.

Meera smiled.

— No.

She looked toward the lights below.

— I just know loneliness when I see it.

For several seconds neither spoke. Then Vardaan quietly asked:

— Do you ever get scared?

— Of what?

— This life.

The empire. The responsibilities. The enemies. The expectations. Everything. Meera thought carefully before answering.

— Every day.

Vardaan looked surprised. She laughed.

—Tum sochte ho sirf tum darte ho?

You think only you feel fear?

Then her expression softened.

— Courage ka matlab dar ka na hona nahi hota.

Courage doesn't mean the absence of fear.

— It means choosing something more important than fear.

The answer stayed with him long after the conversation ended. Because for years, revenge had been the most important thing in his life. Now something else was beginning to take its place. A future. And that terrified him.

Meanwhile, Aarohi found herself unable to enjoy any of the celebrations. Every song sounded distant. Every smile felt fragile. Every happy moment carried a hidden weight. Because she was still carrying the truth. Pratap Chauhan. Her father. A truth capable of destroying everything. Several times she considered telling Vardaan. Several times she walked toward him. Several times she stopped. The timing never felt right. Or perhaps she was simply afraid. Late that evening, she found herself sitting beside *Meera*. The celebrations continued around them. Meera watched the crowd. Then quietly said:

— You look sad.

Aarohi laughed weakly.

— Journalists always look sad or suspicious.

— That's not true.

Meera looked at her carefully.

— People become sad when they're carrying something alone.

The words landed harder than intended. Aarohi immediately looked away. For a moment she wondered if Meera somehow knew everything. But Meera asked no further questions. She simply sat beside her. Sometimes kindness was more dangerous than interrogation. Because kindness lowered defenses. Across the region, invitations continued arriving. Political leaders. Business owners. Village representatives. Former rivals. Old allies. Everyone wanted to attend. The wedding had become an event larger than the family itself. Yet hidden among the invitations and congratulations were quieter developments. Several intelligence sources reported unusual movements across neighboring districts. Unknown intermediaries making contact with forgotten networks. Old loyalties suddenly reawakened. People long believed to be retired, returning to public life. Nothing illegal. Nothing obvious. Nothing that could justify alarm.

Yet experienced observers noticed patterns. Patterns that made them uncomfortable. Raghuveer presented the reports to Vardaan. The latter studied them silently.

— ka hamni ke chinta hokhe ke chahi?

Raghuveer asked. Vardaan considered the question. Then slowly shook his head.

— ho sakela.

— bakir dar aadt na ban ske.

For years they had prepared for disaster every single day. Now, finally, life was offering something different. He refused to surrender that moment. Even if part of him remained cautious.

Meanwhile, far away, Jay Singh Bajwa received news of the wedding. The old kingmaker sat alone in a dimly lit room. The messenger finished speaking. Silence followed. Then Bajwa smiled. Not warmly. Not happily. Almost sadly. Because he understood something few others did. People were most vulnerable when they believed suffering was finally over. Hope created openings that fear never could. He looked toward the window. Winter fog covered the landscape beyond. For several moments he said nothing. Then he quietly spoke:

— har raj girla se pahile jashn manavela.

Nobody in the room responded. Nobody dared.

Back at Bharat Furnace, the wedding day finally arrived. Thousands gathered. Music filled the air. Lights illuminated every corner of the complex. For one evening, the furnace stopped being a symbol of power. It became a symbol of family. Vardaan stood before the gathered crowd. For the first time in years, he wasn't thinking about enemies. Or territory. Or revenge. Only about the woman standing beside him. Meera. The person who had somehow found humanity beneath layers of grief and anger. The ceremonies continued late into the night. Blessings were offered. Promises exchanged. Families reunited. Old wounds temporarily forgotten. Even Aarohi managed to smile. Even Raghuveer relaxed. Even hardened workers allowed themselves to dream. And perhaps that was the true tragedy. Not that danger still existed. But that everyone finally believed they had earned peace.

Near midnight, after most guests had departed, Vardaan and Meera walked alone through the quiet furnace grounds. The lights still glowed. The winter air felt cold. The celebrations had faded into silence. Meera stopped near one of the old furnaces. The same furnace that had witnessed the rise and fall of generations. She looked at him.

— ab kya hoga??

For years, Vardaan always had an answer. A plan. A strategy. A target. Tonight, he simply smiled.

— mujhen nahin pata.

The answer surprised both of them. Then he continued.

— bohot din baad pehli baar...

—...mujhe lag raha hai ki sab theek hai.

Meera laughed softly. And together they continued walking through the sleeping heart of the empire. Above them, the winter sky remained silent. The stars watched. Just as they had watched Vairav. Just as they had watched Vikram. Just as they now watched Vardaan. And somewhere beyond the horizon, unseen forces were already moving toward Bharat Furnace. Toward destiny. But on this night—none of that mattered. On this night, the king was finally happy. And history had always been cruelest to happy men.

CHAPTER THIRTY-FOUR

RED RAIN

Bharat Furnace, January - February, 2022

Winter was dying. The cold winds that had ruled Bihar and Jharkhand for months were beginning to retreat, leaving behind mornings wrapped in fog and afternoons soaked in sunlight. For the first time in years, Bharat Furnace looked less like a fortress and more like a home. The chimneys still roared. The furnaces still burned. Coal trucks still entered and exited through the massive iron gates twenty-four hours a day. But something had changed. The men standing guard on the walls smiled more often. Workers laughed again. Children could be seen running through the workers' colony. For the first time since Vikram Singh's death, hope had returned. And hope was dangerous. Because every empire in history had fallen when it believed the war was over.

Vardaan Singh stood on the balcony overlooking Bharat Furnace. Thousands of workers moved below. Some loaded coal. Some supervised logistics. Some maintained machinery. Every movement below belonged to him. Not legally. Not politically. But undeniably. The Singh Empire had returned. Stronger. Larger. More feared than ever. The transport routes belonged to him. The coal belt belonged to him. The brick industries belonged to him. Even politicians had started asking permission before entering his territories. A couple of years ago he had been a scientist. Now entire districts waited for his decisions before making theirs. He watched silently. Behind him, footsteps approached. Soft. Familiar. Meera.

Without turning around, he smiled.

— Ka haal ba?

Meera wrapped her arms around him.

— Doctor bole baa ki humni ke dhyaan rakhe ke padi.

Vardaan frowned.

— Kaa matlab?

Meera laughed.

— Matlab hum akela na bani.

For a moment Vardaan did not understand. Then realization hit him. The world stopped. The furnaces disappeared. The empire disappeared. The wars disappeared. Everything vanished. Only her words remained. Hum akela na bani. We are not alone anymore. His eyes widened. Meera slowly took his hand and placed it on her stomach. The silence lasted several seconds. Then another. Then another. And suddenly the feared king of the coal belt looked like a lost child.

— Hum...

His voice cracked. Meera smiled.

— Haan.

— Pakki baat?

— Haan.

— Sach?

— Haan.

The smile that appeared on Vardaan's face was something nobody in Bharat Furnace had seen in years. Not the king. Not the mafia. Not the conqueror. Just a man. Just a husband. Just a future father.

The news spread through Bharat Furnace before sunset. By evening the entire empire knew. By nightfall celebrations had begun. Workers distributed sweets. Truck drivers decorated vehicles. Coal miners burst firecrackers. Contractors announced bonuses. Old women blessed Meera. Children ran through the colony shouting:

— Singh ke waaris aawe wala baa!

The heir of the Singh family is coming.

Inside her room, Aarohi watched the celebrations through a window. The sight should have made her happy. Instead it filled her with dread. Because she knew something nobody else knew. Pratap Chauhan was her father. The truth sat inside her like poison. Every day she delayed revealing it. Every day it became heavier. She closed her eyes. For months she had convinced herself she was protecting Vardaan. Now she wasn't sure. Maybe she was protecting herself.

A knock interrupted her thoughts.

— Madam.

She turned.

Ramdeen stood outside. The old man entered slowly. He had become thinner over the last year. Older. More fragile. But his eyes remained sharp. He looked at her. Then at the celebrations outside. Then back at her.

— Dil pareshaan baa?

Aarohi forced a smile.

— Aap sab samajh jaate hain na?

Ramdeen sighed.

— Budha aadmi bani.

Then he became serious.

— Jitna der kariha sach batave mein... utna mushkil hoi.

The words struck her hard. Because she knew he was right.

Hundreds of kilometers away. In an isolated farmhouse near the Jharkhand border. Pratap Chauhan sat alone. The room was dark. Only a single lantern burned. Maps covered the table. Territories. Routes. Supply lines. All marked with red ink. Most of them lost. One by one. Month after month. Year after year. Everything he had built was collapsing. The realization was impossible to ignore now. The war was ending. And he was losing. A young lieutenant entered.

— Bhai ji.

Pratap looked up.

— Kaa ba?

— Bajwa sahib ke log phir aail rahe.

Pratap's eyes narrowed.

— Kaa kahal?

— Bas itna ki intezaar kari.

The lieutenant hesitated.

— Ab hamni ke meeting mein Bajwa sahib ke log humni ke bulawat bhi na.

Silence. Pratap looked away. The lieutenant had unknowingly spoken the truth. Something had changed. For years Jay Singh Bajwa had spoken to him directly. For years every major decision passed through Bajwa. Now messages arrived through intermediaries. Meetings happened without him. Plans were made elsewhere. The realization disturbed him. Maybe he was no longer a partner. Maybe he was becoming expendable.

Late that night. A private gathering took place inside Bharat Furnace. Only inner-circle members attended. Contractors. Union leaders. Political allies. Security chiefs. The most powerful men in the empire. They had come to celebrate. But also to discuss the future. The unborn child changed everything. For the first time in decades there would be another generation. Another heir. Another Singh. The discussions became increasingly emotional. One contractor raised a toast.

— Vikram babu ke baad lagat rahe sab khatam ho gayil.

Another nodded.

— Lekin aaj lagat ba Bhagwan phir se sab shuru hoil baa.

Everyone applauded. Except Vardaan. Because hearing Vikram's name still hurts. Always. Later that night he visited Vikram's memorial alone. The marble structure stood behind Bharat Furnace. Simple. Unadorned. Exactly how Vikram would have wanted. Vardaan placed flowers there. Then sat quietly. For a long time he said nothing. Finally he spoke.

— Bhai...

His voice barely rose above a whisper.

— Hum baap banat bani.

The words broke something inside him. Because Vikram should have been there. Vikram should have seen it. Vikram should have laughed at him. Given advice. Mocked him. Protected him. Instead there was only silence.

Far away. In Chandigarh. Inside a luxurious private estate. Jay Singh Bajwa stood before a giant window. Watching rain fall. Despite his age, he still looked powerful. Still looked dangerous. Still looked like the man who had manipulated half a century of bloodshed. A trusted associate approached.

— Singh Empire jashn karat baa.

Bajwa smiled faintly.

— Haan.

— Meera garbhwati baa.

The associate waited. Bajwa remained silent. Then:

— Sabse aasaan cheez ka hoyela?

The associate looked confused.

— Ji?

Bajwa slowly turned.

— Aadmi ke maarna.

His eyes were cold.

— Sabse mushkil cheez ka hoyela?

The associate remained silent. Bajwa answered himself.

— Umeed ke maarna.

Killing hope. Not people. Hope. That was how empires truly died.

February has arrived. Preparations intensified. A massive baby shower celebration was planned for Holi. Workers demanded it. Union leaders insisted. Entire districts wanted to participate. The event quickly became larger than a family gathering. It became a symbol. The rebirth of the Singh Empire.

One evening Aarohi finally made a decision. No more delays. No more excuses. No more fear. She would tell Vardaan everything. Tonight. She walked toward his office. Heart pounding. Hands trembling. Years of secrets ready to spill. She reached the door. Stopped. Took a deep breath. Then entered. Inside she found Vardaan studying logistics reports. He looked exhausted. Yet strangely peaceful. She opened her mouth.

— Vardaan...

Before she could continue, his phone rang. Then another. Then another. Emergency meetings. Transport issues. Coal permits. Political negotiations. The moment vanished. Again. Hours later Aarohi sat alone. Frustrated. Angry. Terrified. Every time she tried, fate intervened. And somewhere deep inside, a terrible feeling grew. As if time was running out. As if something enormous was approaching. Something unstoppable.

Outside Bharat Furnace, clouds gathered above the night sky. Dark. Heavy. Silent. The first drops of rain began falling over the chimneys. Over the coal yards. Over the roads. Over the empire. Like a warning. Like a prophecy. Like blood preparing to fall from the heavens. The workers called it ordinary rain. The old men called it seasonal weather. But somewhere far away, Jay Singh Bajwa watched the same clouds and smiled. Because he knew something they didn't. The happiest days of the Singh Empire had already begun. And that meant their destruction was finally near.

CHAPTER THIRTY-FIVE

LAAL HOLI

Bharat Furnace, March 2022

The morning arrived wrapped in color. For the first time in years, Bharat Furnace looked less like the headquarters of an empire and more like a festival ground. Red. Yellow. Pink. Green. Thousands of packets of gulal had been distributed throughout the workers' colonies. Coal trucks were decorated with marigold garlands. Children ran through the roads laughing. Women sang folk songs near the furnace yards. Drums echoed across the valley. The entire Singh Empire had gathered. Not for war. Not for business. Not for politics. For family. For hope. For the future. For the child that had not yet been born.

Above the furnace complex stood giant banners. *WELCOME THE HEIR OF THE SINGH EMPIRE.* Workers had painted them by hand. Some crooked. Some uneven. All sincere. Vardaan stood on the balcony overlooking the celebrations. For several moments he simply watched. No meetings. No weapons. No maps. No war. Only people. His people. A strange warmth filled his chest. Something he had almost forgotten existed. Peace.

Behind him, Meera approached. She wore a simple red saree. Her pregnancy had begun to show. Not enough for strangers. Enough for him. Enough for those who loved her. Vardaan looked at her and smiled. The expression came naturally now. Something that had become rare over the years. Meera stood beside him.

— Ka dekh rahe ho?

Vardaan nodded toward the crowd.

— Ee sab.

Meera laughed.

— Ee sab tumhar log baa.

— Na.

He shook his head.

— Hamaar na.

Then he pointed below.

— Vikram bhai ke.

For a brief moment silence fell between them. Meera squeezed his hand. And neither said anything more.

Elsewhere inside Bharat Furnace... Aarohi sat alone. A folded envelope rested on the table before her. Inside it were photographs. Documents. Adoption records. Hospital reports. Everything. The truth. The secret she had carried for months. Pratap Chauhan. Her father. The name stared back at her from every page. Like a curse. Like a wound. Today she had finally decided. No more delays. No more excuses. No more fear. Today she would tell Vardaan everything. After the celebrations. After the rituals. After Meera's happiness. Then she would tell him. Whatever happened afterward... she would accept.

Hundreds of kilometers away... Pratap Chauhan sat inside an abandoned mining warehouse. The once-feared kingpin looked exhausted. The war had aged him. Destroyed him. Most of his territories were gone. Most of his commanders were dead. The empire he had spent years building was collapsing. Maps covered the table before him. Every week another red mark appeared. Another lost district. Another surrendered route. Another betrayal. A lieutenant entered.

— Bhai ji.

Pratap looked up.

— Kaa ba?

— Log kahat baa ki aaj Bharat Furnace mein lakhon ke bheed baa.

Pratap nodded.

— Haan.

The lieutenant hesitated. Then asked:

— Hum attack kari?

Pratap slowly looked at him. Then laughed. A tired laugh. A defeated laugh.

— Naa.

The lieutenant seemed confused. Pratap stood. Walked toward a dusty window. Outside, rain clouds gathered far away.

— Naa.

His voice became quieter.

— Ee hamaar jang na rahe.

The lieutenant frowned.

— Kaa matlab?

Pratap stared into the distance. Because somewhere deep inside... for the first time... he was beginning to understand. Someone else was moving pieces. Someone else was deciding outcomes. Someone else was writing the ending. And it wasn't him.

Far away. Chandigarh. Jay Singh Bajwa watched a live feed from Bharat Furnace. Drone footage. Phone footage. Security footage. Every angle. Every entrance. Every exit. Every blind spot. A trusted operative stood beside him.

— Sab taiyaar baa.

Bajwa nodded. His expression revealed nothing. No joy. No anger. No excitement. Only calculation. Pure calculation. The kind that had destroyed generations. The kind that had built empires from corpses.

Back at Bharat Furnace... The celebrations reached their peak. Drums thundered. Fireworks exploded. Thousands danced. Workers smeared colors onto each other's faces. Children attacked adults with water guns. Coal miners danced beside transport drivers. Old enemies embraced. Young lovers disappeared into crowds. For a few hours... the entire empire forgot violence existed. Then came the baby shower ceremony. A massive stage had been constructed near the old furnace. Decorated with flowers. Lights. Traditional cloth. Workers crowded every rooftop. Every balcony. Every road. Everyone wanted to witness history.

When Meera stepped onto the stage... the crowd erupted. Thousands cheering. Thousands clapping. Thousands blessing her. Many of them had watched Vardaan grow up. Many had worked under Vairav. Many had followed Vikram. To them... this child represented continuity. The future. The next generation. The survival of the Singh name. Vardaan sat beside Meera. For the first time in years... he looked happy. Truly happy. Not victorious. Not powerful. Happy. And that made him vulnerable. Aarohi watched from nearby. The envelope remained inside her bag. She glanced at Vardaan. Then at Meera. Then at the crowd. Not now. She thought. After this, after everything ends. Then I'll tell him.

The first explosion happened at 2:17 PM. Nobody understood what they had heard. First, people assumed it was another firecracker. Another celebration. Another part of the festivities. Then the second explosion came. Much louder. Closer. Violent. A fuel truck erupted into flames near the eastern gate. The blast threw men into the air. Screams followed immediately. For two seconds...nobody moved. Nobody understood. Nobody reacted. Then chaos began. Another explosion. Then another. Then another. The eastern wall collapsed. Vehicles burned. Workers ran in every direction. Children screamed. People fell. People pushed. People disappeared beneath crowds.

Gunfire erupted. Sharp. Precise. Professional. Not gangsters. Not amateurs. Assassins. Vardaan was on his feet instantly. Years of war taking control.

— MEERA!

He grabbed her. Pulled her behind cover. Bodyguards surrounded them. Weapons appeared. Orders exploded.

— Gate band karo!

— Snipers khojo!

— Sab log andar mein jao!

The festival transformed into a battlefield within seconds. Red powder filled the air. Mixed with smoke. Mixed with blood. Creating a horrifying crimson fog. Children searched for parents.Parents searched for children. Workers searched for exits.

Nobody knew where danger was coming from. Because danger was everywhere. Inside the panic...traitors emerged. Hidden operatives. Sleeper agents. Men who had waited years. They began shooting from inside the crowd. The attack had never been intended as a military operation. It was an execution. A massacre. Near the stage...Aarohi saw a sniper positioning himself atop a warehouse roof. Without thinking she grabbed a fallen rifle. Fired. The sniper collapsed. Another assassin emerged. Then another. Then another. Too many. Far too many. This wasn't Pratap's style. She realized it instantly. This was something else. Something larger. Something colder.

Vardaan fought through the chaos. Searching. Shouting. Killing. Protecting. Then he saw it. A single gunman. Hidden inside the crowd. Weapon aimed. Not at him. At Meera. Time slowed. Vardaan screamed.

— MEERAAAA!

The shot rang out. The world froze. Meera staggered. Looked down, blood spreading across her saree. Then another shot. Then another. Her body collapsed. For one terrible second...the crowd became silent. As if reality itself had stopped. Vardaan reached her before she hit the ground. Caught her. Held her. Blood covered his hands instantly. Warm. Endless.

— No...

His voice broke.

— No...

Meera tried to speak. No words came. Only blood. Tears filled her eyes. She looked at him. Not afraid. Not angry. Only sad. As if apologizing. For leaving. Then she placed her hand on her stomach. The gesture shattered him. Because he understood. Immediately. The child. The child. The child. Everything disappeared. The gunfire. The explosions. The screams. The empire. The war. The world. Only her remained. And she was dying.

— Doctor!

He screamed.

— DOCTOR!

But even as he shouted...he already knew. Meera's eyes slowly lost focus. Her hand slipped from his. And the future of the Singh Empire died beside her. The crowd around them became a blur. Vardaan sat motionless. Covered in blood. Covered in Holi colors. Covered in sorrow. Unable to move. Unable to breathe. Unable to think. A king surrounded by thousands. And completely alone. Hours later... The fires still burned. Bodies lined the roads. Ambulances came and went. The dead continued to rise. Nobody knew the final count. Hundreds. Maybe more. The greatest celebration in Singh Empire history had become its greatest tragedy.

Late that evening...Aarohi sat beside Meera's covered body. The envelope remained in her hands. The truth is still hidden inside. She looked toward Vardaan. He hadn't spoken in hours. Hadn't moved. Hadn't cried. Hadn't blinked. Something inside him had broken. Completely. And suddenly she knew. This was no longer the right time. The truth would have to wait. Again. Because the man sitting there wasn't Vardaan anymore. Not the scientist. Not the lover. Not the brother. Not even the king. Something else had been born today. Something darker.

Far away...Pratap Chauhan received the news. He listened silently. Without interruption. Without reaction. When the call ended... he sat alone for several minutes. For the first time...fear entered his eyes. Because if he hadn't ordered it...then only one man could have. Jay Singh Bajwa. And somewhere in Chandigarh... the old kingmaker stared into the night. Watching empires burn. Exactly as he always had.

Outside Bharat Furnace, rain began to fall. Mixing with blood. Mixing with color. Turning the ground crimson. *"Laal Holi"*. Red Holi. The day hope died.

CHAPTER THIRTY-SIX

UNHOLY

Chhoti Holi, The Day After, March 2022

The fires of Bharat Furnace were still burning. Smoke rose from blackened warehouses. Destroyed trucks remained scattered across the roads like broken skeletons. The smell of burnt diesel, gunpowder, wet ash, and death hung over the valley. Hundreds had died. Thousands had witnessed it. Nobody had slept. Nobody had celebrated. Nobody had spoken above a whisper. The Singh Empire had entered mourning. But its king had entered something else.

Inside the central furnace hall, Meera's body rested upon a ceremonial platform draped in white cloth. Flowers surrounded her. Candles burned. Workers came one after another to pay their respects. Many wept openly. Some touched her feet. Others simply folded their hands. No one left without tears.

At the center of the hall sat Vardaan Singh. Motionless. Silent. Still wearing the same clothes. The same blood. His wife's blood. Dried across his hands. Across his face. Across his chest. Hours had passed. He had not eaten. He had not slept. He had not spoken. And he had not washed. Because he had made a vow to himself, a dangerous one.

Ramdeen stood before him.

— Malik...

No response.

— Ab antim sanskaar ke taiyaari kare ke padi.

Nothing. Finally Vardaan lifted his eyes. Cold. Dead. Empty.

— Dah-sanskaar tab hoi.

His voice was barely human.

— Jab ee sab ke zimmedaar mar jaayi.

Silence.

The old man understood. This was no longer grief. This was judgment. Word spread through Bihar and Jharkhand before sunrise. The King had spoken. The hunt had begun. By morning every loyal commander had gathered. Coal operators. Transport chiefs. Brick contractors. Former gang leaders. Village strongmen. Political allies. Everyone. Inside the war room, a giant map covered the wall. Red markers. Black markers. Enemy safe houses. Weapon depots. Transport routes. Pratap's remaining territories. Vardaan entered. The room fell silent. Every man present instinctively lowered his eyes. Not from respect. From fear. Because something had changed. The man entering the room was not the same Vardaan they had followed for two years. The scientist was gone. The husband was gone. Even the king seemed gone. Only rage remained.

— Pratap kahan ba?

Nobody answered immediately. Finally one commander stepped forward.

— Teen jagah ke khabar baa.

— Sab bata.

Maps unfolded. Coordinates appeared. Safe houses identified. Movement patterns analyzed. Within minutes the largest operation in Singh Empire history was underway. The retaliation began before noon. Convoys rolled out from Bharat Furnace. Hundreds of vehicles. Thousands of armed men. Coal trucks converted into armored carriers. Transport fleets converted into war machines. The entire empire moved as one.

By afternoon the first target fell. A warehouse complex near Dhanbad. Pratap's men never saw them coming. The gates exploded inward. Gunfire erupted. Defenders scattered. Within twenty minutes the compound belonged to Vardaan. Then another. Then another. Then another. By sunset seven major strongholds had fallen. Pratap's network was collapsing faster than anyone believed possible. Because this was no longer a territorial war. This was extermination.

Meanwhile... Pratap Chauhan was running. For the first time in twenty years. Running. Every phone call brought worse news. Every report carried another disaster, every commander lost, every route captured, every hideout compromised. Inside an abandoned quarry near the Jharkhand border, he listened quietly. No anger. No panic. Only exhaustion.

One lieutenant finally exploded.

— Bhai ji! Kuch kari!

Pratap looked at him.

— Kaa kari?

— Hamla kari!

Pratap laughed bitterly.

— Kispe?

Nobody answered. Because they all knew. The war was over. For years they had feared Vardaan Singh. Today they feared something worse. A man with nothing left to lose. Night arrived. Rain began falling again. The same rain that had fallen during Holi.

Near midnight a convoy stopped outside the factory on the quarry. One of Pratap's final safe houses. Vardaan stepped out. Rifle in hand. Blood is still staining his clothes. Rain washing over him, unable to clean, unable to cleanse him. The factory was surrounded within minutes. Floodlights ignited. Escape routes sealed. Snipers deployed.

A commander approached.

— Mil gaya.

Vardaan nodded once. Then walked inside. The building was almost empty. Most men had fled. Others surrendered. Some fought. Those who fought died. At the far end of the structure sat Pratap Chauhan. Alone. Waiting. No bodyguards. No weapons. No escape. Only two old enemies. At the end of the road. For several moments neither spoke. Rain hammered the roof. Water dripped through broken concrete. The factory echoed with silence. Finally Vardaan spoke.

— Tohar wajah se.

His voice shook.

— Hamaar bhai maral.

No response.

— Hamaar ghar ujral.

Silence.

— Hamaar bachcha maral.

Pratap lowered his eyes. Then Vardaan stepped forward.

— Meera mar gayi.

The words broke. For the first time since the massacre. His voice cracked. Pratap closed his eyes. Pain flashed across his face. Real pain. Not fear. Not guilt. Pain.

— Ee ham na karawle rahe.

Vardaan immediately struck him. A brutal punch. Blood exploded from Pratap's mouth. He fell. Again. Again. Again. Years of hatred. Years of grief. Years of rage. Released through fists. Nobody intervened. Nobody dared. Finally Vardaan stopped. Breathing heavily. Pratap lay bleeding on the floor. Then quietly he spoke.

— Agar hum karawle rahit...

Blood dripped from his lips.

— Ta hum aaj yahan baithal na rahit.

Something in his voice felt different. Not defensive. Not manipulative. Truthful. For the first time...Vardaan listened. And Pratap began talking. About Vikram. About Vairav. About Bharat Furnace. About old betrayals. Old loyalties. Old wounds. Then finally came the truth.

— Hum kabhu raja na rahe.

Pratap laughed sadly.

— Hum hamesha sipahi rahe.

I was never the king. I was always a soldier. The room became silent. Pratap revealed decades of manipulation. Half-truths. Lies. Manufactured betrayals. Manufactured hatred. Every road led to one name. Jay Singh Bajwa. The architect. The strategist. The survivor. The man who benefited every time blood was spilled.

Vardaan stood motionless. Trying to process it. Trying to reject it. Trying to believe it.

Then another voice entered. Aarohi. She had arrived during the confrontation. And heard everything. Pratap turned. Their eyes met. For a moment time stopped, Vardaan understood nothing. Father. Daughter. Neither knows how to bridge decades of separation. Pratap stared at her. Then slowly whispered:

— Aarohi...

Tears filled his eyes. The first tears anyone had ever seen. Aarohi froze. Because the emotion was real. Terrifyingly real. Not a gangster. Not a murderer. A father.

— Hum samjhle rahni tu mar gayilu.

His voice broke completely. The room became painfully silent. Every hatred suddenly became more complicated. Every certainty became less certain. Aarohi cried. But said nothing. Because there were no words large enough for this moment. Pratap smiled weakly. A sad smile. A broken smile. Then he looked at Vardaan.

— Ab samjha...

He coughed blood.

— Hum sab mohre rahni.

We were all pieces on the board. Then came gunfire. A single shot. From outside. Everyone turned. Too late. A sniper round tore through Pratap's chest. The room erupted. Weapons raised. Men rushed outside. Chaos exploded. But the sniper had already vanished. Pratap collapsed. Blood spread across the concrete floor. His final breaths came quickly. He looked once more at Aarohi. Then at Vardaan. And whispered:

— Jay Singh Bajwa...

A cough. More blood.

— Sab ke barbaad kailas...

He destroyed all of us. Then the mighty Pratap Chauhan died. The factory fell silent. Outside... The rain intensified. Hours later... The funeral pyre was prepared. Meera lay surrounded by flowers. The entire Singh Empire gathered. This time Vardaan stood. At last. He lit the pyre himself. Flames rose toward the sky. Consuming wood. Consuming flowers. Consuming dreams. Only after the fire had fully taken hold did he walk toward the river. For the first time since Holi... he washed. The blood finally left his hands. But not his soul. Behind him, Aarohi approached. Tears are still visible. There was one final truth. One final wound.

— Vardaan...

He turned. She looked directly into his eyes.

— Pratap Chauhan...

A long pause.

— Mera baap tha.

Silence. The river flowed. The fire burned. The night watched. And Vardaan understood. Nobody had won. Nobody. Not him. Not Pratap. Not Aarohi. Not Vikram. Only one man had won. For decades. Jay Singh Bajwa. Vardaan slowly turned toward the distant glow of Bharat Furnace. The birthplace of the empire. The graveyard of his family. His voice emerged low and cold.

— Pratap ke maar ke hum sochni jang khatam ho gayil.

The wind carried the words across the river.

— Ab samajh mein aawat ba...

His eyes hardened.

— Jang ta ab shuru bhayil ba.

The war has only begun. Far away... In another state. Inside another empire. Jay Singh Bajwa sat alone. Watching the same rain fall beyond his window. For the first time in decades...someone was coming for him. And this time...it was personal.

What Lies Ahead

Vardaan Singh believes he finally knows his enemy.

He is wrong.

The bloodshed that consumed his family did not begin with Pratap Chauhan. It began decades earlier, with secrets buried beneath coal mines, broken oaths, and a betrayal so profound that it shattered three generations of lives.

In Laal Holi Mein Unholy: Vikram, the story travels back in time to reveal the life of Vikram Singh—the brother Vardaan loved, the king his people worshipped, and the man history never truly understood. Through friendship, loyalty, and betrayal, the truth behind his murder slowly emerges.

But the deepest wounds lie even further in the past.

www.ingramcontent.com/pod-product-compliance
Lightning Source LLC
LaVergne TN
LVHW100306210926
848480LV00003B/1039